FOR DUNCAN SHAUL BOCK

the undiscovered country

I see Hermes, unsuspected, dying, well-belov'd, saying to the people *Do not weep for me,*
This is not my true country, I have lived banish'd from my true country.
I now go back there,
I return to the celestial sphere where every one goes in his turn.

WALT WHITMAN

the undiscovered country

S A M A N T H A   G I L L I S O N

GROVE PRESS / *New York*

Published simultaneously in Canada
Printed in the United States of America

FIRST EDITION

Library of Congress Cataloging-in-Publication Data

Gillison, Samantha.

The undiscovered country / Samantha Gillison.

p.   cm.

ISBN 0-8021-1627-2

I. Title.

PS3557.I3945U53   1998

813'.54—dc21   97-40368

Design by Laura Hammond Hough

Grove Press

841 Broadway

New York, NY 10003

98 99 00 01 10 9 8 7 6 5 4 3 2 1

the undiscovered country

part one

Four men from Buni village and a tall American walked up the ridge of Mt. Batani. The New Guinean men were quiet while they climbed, navigating the roots and rocks that sprawled across the trail, breathing in the early morning mist. They did not explain to Masta George where they were going because they knew he knew already: the missionary was their ancestor who had traveled back from the ghost world to their village, and although death had bleached his skin of color and grotesquely elongated his limbs, he was one of them.

At mid-morning they stopped at a clearing near the Kaho river. The New Guineans took bamboo flutes out of a net bag and carefully propped them up on a rock. The flutes, brown with smoke from the years they had been hidden in the rafters of the men's house, were tattooed with burned-in patterns. The men began to gather long ginger leaves and red orchids, and Masta George stood alone in the clearing, smiling self-consciously, gazing at the shafts of pure sunlight that poured out onto the forest's moss-covered floor.

The men wove the greenery and flowers into crowns and placed them low on their foreheads and then lifted the flutes to their lips and began to play. At first they played the songs of the bird spirits, and then the lament of First Mother when her son cut off her penis, and finally the song of the wounded warrior, dying alone in the rain forest. The throbbing, rhythmic tones encircled the missionary and filled the trees, swallowing the sounds around them so that eventually even the roaring Kaho was obscured.

And after they stopped, when Masta George began to ask questions about the flutes, they were puzzled. Why was he pretending not to know? But it was then that the missionary shook his head and told them that the flutes were from the devil. Playing them, keeping them a secret from the women and children, was pagan. They must no longer do this evil thing, he said in his Texas-accented Pisin, or they would burn in hellfires forever.

The men walked down the mountain distressed, unspeaking, clutching the flutes that Masta George would not let them put back in their net bag. When they arrived in the main hamlet of Buni village, a crowd gathered around them. Masta George shouted: "Blow the bamboo! Show your families what evil you have been doing hidden away in the bush!"

The men began to play in tandem, quietly at first, but then louder until the eerie sound filled the human settlement. For the first time in any of their lives, in any of the villagers' memories, the sacred flutes were played in front of women and children and uninitiated boys far from the shelter of the rain forest canopy or the dark, smoke-filled men's house.

When they stopped playing, they stacked the flutes on the ground. Masta George knelt down and held a Red Head match to the pile of dried bamboo and as the flutes caught fire and burned, he stood up and preached. He said that they had saved themselves from the coming solar eclipse: he smiled and spread his arms out at the women and old men and children

who gaped at him. He said that day would continue to follow night as tes-
tament to Jesus Christ's love for Papua New Guinea.

The afternoon rain finally came, and the crowd rushed away, inter-
rupting the missionary's sermon. The raindrops pounded the packed orange
earth and filled the air with heavy moisture. And while Masta George peered
at them from under the thatch roof of the mission rain shelter, the men stood
staring at the extinguished pyre, unable to leave, watching as the rain washed
the ashes of the flutes into the flood gutters that encircled the hamlet.

O N E

In Cuzco, the child got sick from the altitude. Her parents stayed with her there, in the small hotel room, and wiped the sour-smelling sweat off her skin with a washcloth. They smoothed her hair back when she vomited spit and pink Dramamine onto the floor, and later they changed the hotel's worn, flower-patterned sheets when she peed in the bed. And it wasn't until the third day that her mother opened the heavy wood shutters that covered the window. The smoke of roasting meat and cold air and distant voices speaking Spanish blew in. Her parents sat looking at the sky, breathing the outside world into their lungs, and discussed what they might do: they had planned to see this country.

The two of them drew straws, and in the morning the man, Peter, went off alone. When he came back, he told his wife how the train to Machu Picchu had rocked back and forth on its tracks. He said that he sat next to Indians who smelled of wool tannin and sweat and smoked cigarettes and were silent as the train ambled through the dark green landscape. He said that the ruins were bright in the haze of the mid-morning sun and hurt his eyes and that he felt terrible when he stood there alone, gazing at them. But what he did not tell her was that when he left that morning, he had been relieved to get away from the hotel room, and for the first hour on the train he sat across from an Indian woman who was heavyset and had beautiful, thick hair that she wore in braids under a black felt hat. He did not say that when he was at Machu Picchu, he had put his mouth to the walls and tasted the stone of the Inca monuments.

And when he got back, the two of them went to the hotel's dining room to talk about his trip, and they drank coffee and ate sweet rolls and smoked. They stayed there for a long time, interrupting their conversation to watch the rush of white-shirted waiters laden with heavy trays move over plush, red carpeting. As they talked, they decided to leave the mountains; the girl was too sick. They both felt badly because they had argued about her being too young to travel like this before they left Boston, and now Peter said: "It's just being here, at this altitude, that's all. She'll be better as soon as we leave."

The next morning his wife, June, bought plane tickets and cabled her bank, and by the afternoon they were able to fly to San Miguel island. June booked them a cottage at a hotel that looked out on the beach through screen-covered windows. A huge palm tree grew outside their door, and its grotesque branched roots sprayed out to a broken-up cement path that was set in the sandy earth. Taylor felt better when they got to the beach, and she drank two bottles of Colombian soda pop that stained her lips and tongue deep red. She went swimming with her father in the dark ocean.

"Say good-bye to the Atlantic, Taytie," Peter said as they stood together in shallow water. He was relieved that she wasn't sick anymore. He had been miserable about her in Peru, but now, for the first time since they left Boston, he was excited about getting to the field. He watched his daughter cup her little hands and scoop seawater up to her face, and he thought: we never should have brought her.

"We're leaving this ocean," he said. "We're leaving this hemisphere." Peter stretched his arms out as if he were embracing the horizon.

"Good-bye," Taylor called out, and her quiet voice bothered Peter. He knew she was trying to please him, so he smiled at her. Then he looked across the bay and saw how the beach in the distance was enormous and iridescent in the afternoon light.

...

Later, when she was in the field, the days on San Miguel were the only part of their trip to New Guinea that was vivid to June. And even at the time the details of the island were sharp-edged and clear to her: the hotel maid who was short and pretty and missing her front teeth, and the breakfast tray she brought them, covered with plates of fried eggs and salt ham, glasses of papaya juice, and wide bowls of café con leche.

There, in their cottage that was full of filtered sunlight and ocean-heavy air, Peter went through his field supplies, repacking the sterile, plastic-capped syringes, glass test tubes, boxes of slides, and pill bottles with their neatly typed labels. He even pulled out his microscope and swaddled it in bubble wrap, strapping it to the sides of its leather case. June felt compelled to watch as he went through the medical supplies, and she sat silent, lighting him cigarettes, dizzy from his slow, methodical movements. She could not believe what they were doing. And although she saw how Peter was determined with his instruments and field guides, she thought: we might turn around. Boston was still strong in her consciousness.

"I want to help, you know, Peter. When we get there," she said.

Her husband nodded his head and smiled at her. "I know," he said. "I want you to."

That night when the three of them were in the cottage, and June could hear from her bed that Taylor was sleeping, she masturbated and then woke Peter up, searching his back and thighs with her fingers, breathing in the smell of his skin. She kissed him with her tongue, tasting the sleep breath in his mouth, and as he stirred, she cupped her breast with his hand.

"What?" he asked, drowsy, half awake.

"Peter," she whispered, "are you sleeping?"

She could feel him smiling; he wrapped his arms around her, and as she moved close against his chest, he fell back into sleep. She was awake then, and lay there with her hand on his warm belly and listened to her daughter's even breathing and the swells that came in from the gulf and crashed against the San Miguel beach.

...

The last night on the island an English couple, Harry and Veronica Lapham, came and sat with them at the hotel's dining room for dinner. The Laphams were retired, they said, traveling the world on their savings. Veronica Lapham had short gray hair and faint lines scored into the delicate skin around her mouth and eyes. She peered over at June as they ate.

"Can we buy you an after-dinner drink?" she asked.

"Oh, no," June said. Veronica Lapham made her uncomfortable: she didn't like the way the woman had invaded their dinner and then insisted on how lovely Taylor was, how beautiful San Miguel was, and how marvelous it was for them all to be there. She wanted to get away from them and go back to the cottage.

She looked at Peter, hopefully, and said, "We're leaving in the morning."

"Come on, how about just one," Mrs. Lapham urged, smiling. "You'll still make the plane."

Peter laughed and agreed that they could have just one and make the flight in the morning. So, the five of them stayed sitting on the dining room's patio that was decorated with strings of blinking Christmas lights. June watched Peter as he leaned back into his chair.

He began to talk about his fieldwork and she was surprised. He didn't usually talk like this with strangers. It must be the gin, she thought. Mr. Lapham raised his eyebrows. "Quite impressive," he said.

"Not really," Peter said. "I'm just another doctoral student. I've got an exotic locale to examine my specimens in is all."

"Are you looking for anything in particular?" Mrs. Lapham asked him.

"Well," Peter said. "I've been studying samples of this organism, a blood-borne parasite that's peculiar to the region we're going to, in the lab at Harvard. I want to see how it behaves in the population—if it's affecting things like birth weight and morbidity. But I'm also interested in seeing what else emerges from the data—from a carefully gathered sampling of a population in a completely remote village."

"He's got a theory," June said.

"Have you?" Mr. Lapham said, smiling.

"Yes, a few," Peter said and laughed.

June's face reddened and she looked down at her hands.

"How lovely that you're able to spend some time seeing the world on your way to New Guinea," Mrs. Lapham said, looking at June with friendly concern.

"Yes," June said, looking up at the woman. "I thought'd be nice."

Mr. Lapham ordered another round of drinks. Taylor wandered away from them and sat on the edge of the deck, looking out into the dark distance.

"How much longer are you three traveling for?" Mr. Lapham asked.

"A few more weeks," Peter said. "But actually," he paused and looked over at his daughter, "I'm getting restless. I'm sort of ready to get to the field."

June stared at him.

"Ah, the vigor of youth," Mr. Lapham said.

"I didn't know you weren't enjoying yourself," June said sharply. "If you're not having fun, let's just cancel the rest of the trip and fly straight to Port Moresby."

"June," Peter said. "That's not what I meant. Come on, we're just talking here." He held his arms out and smiled at the Laphams. He looked at his wife and realized that he was in the same place he always got with her. Backing up, apologizing, was no better than standing his ground.

June got up from the table. She walked over to Taylor and put her hand on the girl's shoulder. She looked over at her husband and for a moment it seemed as though she would say something, but she didn't. She just walked across the patio past the empty tables and then down the steps, into the darkness with her daughter beside her.

Mrs. Lapham looked after June and Taylor. "I'm so sorry," she said. "We shouldn't have foisted our company on you."

"No, no," Peter said. "We've just had a rough time in Peru with Taylor. The altitude was very hard on her."

"Traveling is so stressful," she said.

"She's fine," Peter said. He thought about June walking with Taylor along the path to their cottage. "She's just tired," he said.

He stayed at the restaurant and ordered a whiskey and ginger ale, and felt the pleasant wind blow through the palms and up onto the patio. When he said good night, he thought that he liked this couple, and he was sorry that June had acted the way she did. He walked past the shabby cottages, listening to the ocean and the lazy sounds of people getting ready to go to sleep. He knew that June was awake, waiting for him, hurt. He had known she didn't want to stay there, drinking after dinner, but he was tired, and he didn't feel like fighting with her.

"Why did you say that in front of those horrible people?" June asked him when he walked inside.

"June," Peter whispered. He saw that Taylor was asleep, frowning with her mouth open.

"I just wish you hadn't said that, about wanting to get to New Guinea already, in front of them."

"It's nothing. I'm just excited about going to the field."

"Well, then, why don't we just go? This isn't cheap, you know, this little jaunt around the world."

"No, I know that," he said. "You've made that quite clear."

He lay down on the bed and kicked his shoes off. He closed his eyes.

"I'm sorry," he said. "Really. I just wanted a drink. Everything doesn't have to be so, so—" he stopped and yawned. He knew that if he didn't say something kind to her, she would be awake, upset, figuring out the argument and his words all night. Maybe it was already too late, he thought. It didn't matter what he said. "I'm sorry," he repeated.

June stared at him. It always amazed her that he could go to sleep in the midst of an argument.

"Peter," she said.

"Try to sleep," he said and did not open his eyes.

"I can't," she said. She was crying again, quietly, wiping the back of her hand on the bedspread.

"Take a valium," he said, sleepily. He was reaching into the dark folds of his consciousness, willing everything away from his mind.

"I hate that stuff," she said. "I can taste metal in my mouth when I take it."

But he was gone, and she was alone in the room with the sleeping bodies of her husband and child. She stood at the window and breathed in the heavy, salt-filled air. She was still, watching for the dawn to break. After a while she realized that it was much too early for light. The expanse of time that stretched between her and the day seemed enormous.

June moved away from the window and turned the light on. The fluorescent bulb snapped and then filled the room with its glow, flattening everything in front of her. She pulled an Agatha Christie from her bag and sat at the little table and smoked. She flipped through the book, skipping through the pages, reading only the first sentence of a paragraph, and then she turned to the end and read the last page. She thought about waking up the clerk and placing a call to her mother in Boston.

But then, it was too much to think about her mother when she was so upset. Instead, she walked out of the cottage, leaving the light on in the hope that it would wake Peter. She went toward the beach, guided by the low-burning citronella torches that stood along the path. She had planned this trip, and now she felt ridiculous, as though she were dragging Peter and Taylor around with her.

The image of her father came into her being, and she stopped walking and waited for him to pass out of her. She could not shake him, though. His presence became as strong and real as the night air and the inky sea. She was irritated by her own self-pity, and she lit a cigarette and sucked it in, pleased at the taste of the tar on her teeth and lips and tongue. It occurred to her that her father's money confused her so that she couldn't see herself, and all of her plans, all of her ideas, felt foolish. He had left her too much when he died, she thought, and she felt full from it.

June was even awkward in her body; she felt ugly now, her calves and backside flat and heavy, her big breasts uncomfortable in the hot climate. She sweat constantly, and the smell from her armpits and groin was strong, and on this trip when the three of them were in cars or small rooms together, she worried that Peter was revolted by her odor. And she apologized too often. She saw how her incessant sorry-saying was wrong and made them both uneasy. Of course, Peter had been forced on this trip—how could he refuse? or even say what he wanted, since she planned it and paid for it and presented it to him. But how horrible, she thought. I wanted to please him.

She was distracted as she walked into the surf so that she only felt its cold, soft salt in a distant part of her soul. She lit another cigarette and walked down the beach, smoking and pushing against the water, until she was chest high in it. Her cigarette hissed in the foam as she dropped it, and then she began to swim, weighted down by her wet clothes. She swam close to the shore because she was afraid of the opaque water and the nocturnal animals that she imagined were in there with her, swarming under her kicking legs. Soon though, she relaxed and felt only the pull of the waves, and her own breath, and the motion forward.

June was cold as she left the water. She was glad to sit down and watch the sea as the dawn finally broke. The sky filled with gray, and then a thick pinkness seemed to pour from the clouds and settle on top of the water. She lay down and stretched her arms out, burrowing her fingers into the sand. We'll just go straight through to Port Moresby, she thought. That settles that. She wanted to go back to the cottage to pack for their flight. We must be leaving soon, she thought. But then she was so tired and her body was heavy and her lungs filled with ocean air. As she fell into a shallow sleep on the beach, covered in cold, damp clothes, with the sand all over her, making her neck and hands and feet itch, she imagined the sea swelling and crawling up under her, and then she dreamed of bobbing in its waves.

When she woke up a few hours later, she did not know where she was until she stood up and the roar of the ocean shocked her. Her clothes had dried stiff and full of salt and sand. She put her hand to her matted hair. She wanted to wash; she craved cool, fresh water.

A group of the hotel's maids were walking down the beach, holding their shoes in their hands, stepping into the waves as they broke on the sand. They looked wonderful to June in their black dresses and white aprons. Even from far away she could see their bright pink lipstick and that they were laughing, enjoying their walk through the morning to work. All of a sudden June realized that they would see her soon. She was upset that she looked so terrible. What could she say to these women who were so clean and beautiful? She stood there, flustered, and thought halfheartedly that she could joke that she had washed up on the shore from a shipwreck. She put her hands to her face and rubbed the sand and sleep from her eyes.

But the women pretended they didn't see her and went up, off the beach to the head of the cement path that crisscrossed the hotel's grounds. She followed them at a distance, listening to them laugh and the rapid Spanish they spoke that she could barely understand.

June stopped when she got to the door of her cottage and stood there, staring as the maids disappeared into the palm trees and scrubby hibiscus plants that framed the now familiar path to the dining hall. In the moment before she walked into the cottage she closed her eyes and wished that she had never left home.

T W O

The overhead fans at the Port Moresby airport stirred the wet heat, mixing the jet fuel fumes that drifted in from the tarmac with grease from the deep-frying beef patties in the snack shop. Pearl McGuire was eight months pregnant and uncomfortable from the already muggy morning and the hard plastic chairs in the waiting room. She hadn't wanted the chore of picking up this American family, and she tried to remember what her husband had told her about them—their girl was young, six or seven, too young, she had thought, to be dragged into the bush, and the man was from Harvard—some sort of research—she couldn't remember exactly. Their plane was late, and by the time Pearl saw the three of them walking across the tarmac toward the customs hallway, she felt ill, as though she might faint.

But she stood up and made her way to the man, who was tall and blond, and explained that her husband, Steve, whom they had been expecting to see, was with some German doctors in Wewak until the weekend.

"Welcome to Port Moresby, anyway," she said.

They looked exhausted and confused. Pearl was too uncomfortable and self-conscious about her huge belly to make small talk, and she stood next to June Campbell and her daughter while Peter loaded their expensive-looking luggage and boxes of field supplies into the Jeep. So that's the way it is, she thought; they have some money.

She could tell that they were alarmed by the heat and humidity after their long air-conditioned plane ride—everyone was. It took a few hours of sweating before Moresby slowed a person's blood and thoughts down.

"Don't worry," she said as she eased behind the steering wheel, "it's not like this in the Highlands."

Pearl began driving. She was embarrassed by Moresby when people first arrived, as though it were somehow her fault. When her mother came to visit, Pearl had stayed in bed with a migraine headache for three days, unable to bear even the sound of footsteps on the floor. She glanced over at June and saw that she was dressed in a heavy denim skirt and shirt. No one told the woman what to expect, she'd wager. It was always like that with scientists' wives. Well, no one comes here for a holiday, Pearl reasoned—they must know that.

The Jeep groaned up the hill, and Pearl tried to see Moresby with their unaccustomed, American eyes: the precarious-looking houses built up off the ground out of aluminum siding, the too-dry orange earth, the aggressive heat that penetrated every gesture and thought. Peter and June turned their heads when they passed some New Guinean women dressed in *meri* blouses and bright lap laps.

"They're not like your blacks, are they?" Pearl asked.

Peter was staring at a woman standing in the shade with a net bag full of sweet potato hanging off her head, her bare feet and ankles covered in orange dust.

"No, I guess not," he said.

"They're not African, is why," she said. "They're Asian."

Peter nodded and looked away from the woman on the road.

"But they all look different from each other," Pearl said. "Highlanders look nothing like Papuans, who look nothing like Trobriand Islanders, who look nothing like the folks from New Britain." She smiled. "You'll see."

Pearl pulled the Jeep around a steep corner and then stopped in front of a high stucco wall. Bright pink bougainvillea spilled over the top, and two skinny koi dogs lay panting in the ditch that ringed the wall.

"Y'can leave your bags in the Jeep. Gideon'll get them," Pearl said.

The Campbells followed her as she opened a door that was cut out of the thick cement wall. And all of a sudden they were in an arbor of flowering jasmine, frangipani, and hibiscus. Pearl heard June draw her breath in and murmur, "Oh, how lovely." The house was built up on a hillside and looked down on the aluminum roofs that stretched to the water. The Pacific glinted flat in the sunlight, and a cockatoo shrieked at them.

A New Guinean man, shirtless, with a blue lap lap wrapped around his waist and a tall, red-brown afro came out of the house.

"Mornin," he said to Pearl.

"Mornin, Gideon," she said. *"Kago bilon Masta istap arasait. Kisim i kam."*

Gideon nodded his head, and Peter smiled and nodded as the man walked past them.

"Oh, look, Taytie," June said and pointed to an enormous cage full of cockatoos, parrots, and sugar eaters that was built into the underside of the house. The birds were absurd colors: bright green, orange, purple, yellow, and brilliant red. They fluttered about their perches calling to each other, filling the afternoon with a high-pitched ka-kaw-ka-kaw sound. The girl scrutinized the birds.

"Would you like to help me feed them later?" Pearl asked.

But Taylor stepped back and shook her head no, and put her arm around her mother's leg. Pearl was annoyed then, standing in front of the wire mesh wall that Gideon had built for her birds. Taylor stood there looking at her with—what was it? Pearl couldn't tell, but it was rude, and it made her wish she hadn't asked.

"She's just shy," June said. "I'm sure she'd love to help you feed your birds."

"Well, let's show you the pool, shall we?" Pearl said, trying to keep the irritation out of her voice.

Their child has no manners, she thought. She wondered if they realized how lucky they were that Steve had offered to put them up. Most people's entry to Moresby was a lot rougher than this. As she walked ahead of them, they saw down to the small house where Gideon lived. His wife, Lidini, was outside, squatting in front of a fire, boiling a pan of rice. She smiled, and Pearl waved at her distractedly—she was still thinking about the Campbells and their child. They bothered her, all three of them. They were so smug, she thought, and then it occurred to her that maybe this was just the way it was with Americans.

Pearl was proud of the swimming pool—it was lovely, built into the ground at the far end of the house, positioned so that you could look out at town and the ocean while you swam. Pearl had

planted huge pots that overflowed with sweet pea and English hy-
brid roses and placed them around the deck.

"This is fabulous," Peter said.

"Yes, well," Pearl laughed, "Steve and I've tried to make this
place more livable."

"Oh, it seems very livable," Peter said and smiled.

"Does it?" Pearl asked. "Moresby's so dreadful. You'll be glad
you're headed for the Highlands."

She was despondent, and she didn't want to be, not in front
of these people. It was the heat at the airport, she thought, and Taylor
acting as though the birds were dirty and frightening that had unset-
tled her. She hated living in Port Moresby. She looked at the child
who was standing at the edge of the pool.

"Why don't you go for a swim?" she said finally.

...

For the next few days Pearl drove Peter down to the hospital after
breakfast and then went to town, leaving June and Taylor alone
at her house. She went shopping and then stopped by the club
and had lunch with some friends, or, if no one else was there, she
sat on the deck by the water and drank lemonade and listened to
Radio Australia until just before teatime, when she went to get
Peter.

She tried to avoid being alone with June for most of that week,
and when they were all together at dinner or in the early morning,
she was uncomfortable with the way the Campbells clung to each
other. Peter was always watching his wife, with an emotion that
wasn't love, exactly, but was maybe worry. Whatever it was, it
bothered her since she liked him much more than his moody wife,
and he could never really focus on any conversation they had, even
when June wasn't there.

And in the afternoons, when she picked Peter up from the
hospital's laboratory building and drove him back to her house, the

two of them walked outside to find mother and child floating on their backs in the pool or Taylor sprawled over her mother's lap while June smoked and looked out at the view. Pearl watched Peter then: he was so careful, delicate almost, the way he changed into his bathing suit and inserted himself into the quiet hum between mother and daughter.

Pearl was flustered by their unself-conscious intimacy, although in some remote part of her being she realized that there was something odd between them. Peter was too solicitous of his wife, and he was strange with the girl—they were so different from a normal Australian family. But nonetheless, she felt how strongly they wanted to be alone, and she went to the kitchen and listened through the window while June read to Peter from her book and then splashed about the pool, swimming with him and Taylor until dinner. It wasn't right, Pearl thought. They made her feel as though she were intruding in her own home.

...

The day before Steve was getting back, Pearl was too exhausted to go to town and escape her houseguests. She gave Peter the keys to the Jeep and dozed by the pool. She was half aware of June and Taylor eating their breakfast on the deck above her and then coming down the stairs. She woke up and saw that Taylor was playing in the pool by herself while June read. Pearl thought about the child alone in a remote Highlands village for a year. Most of the whites she knew in-country (except for missionaries, of course) sent their children to boarding school while they were in the field, although Taylor was a bit young for that. But still, government people in Port Moresby arranged for even their youngest children to spend a portion of the year with family in Australia. They don't know a thing about this country, Pearl thought. The realization pleased her, but she felt sorry for them, too.

It was strange that the two of them didn't resemble each other, but then there was an air about the child that was exactly like her mother. Pearl looked over at June. She knew that her round, black, plastic sunglasses were fashionable, but they didn't look right. The glasses hid June's eyes and cheeks and emphasized her lips. It was disturbing to look at her when she had them on, since there was always something going into her mouth: she was smoking, or eating, or biting her nails, or drinking from her cup of coffee.

"Did you have an easy pregnancy?" Pearl asked, breaking the quiet.

"Oh, no," June said and put her hand on her belly. "It was very difficult."

"It's bloody awful being so enormous in this heat," Pearl said. This was what she talked about with the women at the club. The heat. She thought that June wasn't listening.

"Oh, yes," June said. "I can see that it would be."

"We're leaving for Sydney as soon as Steve gets back."

"Are you?"

"Yes, of course. To have the baby."

"Don't you want to have your baby here?" June asked.

"You can't have a baby here—where do you think you are?" Pearl was staring at June, disbelieving. "The hospitals here aren't for getting sick in, they're for doing what your husband does—research. You've got to get to Australia when there's anything serious."

June nodded her head and was quiet for a while. "Well, what about all the New Guinean women? What do they do?" she asked.

"The native women die like flies. They have babies and they die." Pearl could hear how she was shouting, but she couldn't stop. "It's not a nice life for these people, you know. What is that saying? Life is brutal, ugly, and short. Make no mistake, that's what a native's life is—brutal, ugly, and short."

They were quiet then, and Pearl felt awkward. She wished that Steve weren't away. Being around the Campbells made her disordered and frantic, the way she had been when she first arrived in New Guinea herself. She shut her eyes.

"Are your dreams very bad?" June asked.

"Sorry?" Pearl said.

"My dreams were so bad when I was pregnant that I never wanted to sleep. And the funny thing is, they weren't usually that frightening or weird when I woke up and thought about them. But I was terrified while I had them."

"Really?" Pearl asked, uninterested.

She shifted and thought about the swelling, the ache in her back and legs, the excruciating hemorrhoids that made her unable to bear being inside her own body. She had a glimpse of June's pregnancy, spent in luxury—air conditioning, pills to keep away the morning sickness, sleeping through afternoons in a familiar, comfortable home, thick soft pillows placed gently under her sore, swollen legs. Imagine dreams being the worst thing about a pregnancy, she thought. Pearl turned away so that June wouldn't see the expression on her face.

"I dreamed of Taylor, too, of course. I mean I saw her in my womb, staring at me with those big blue eyes," June continued. "And I dreamed that she was deformed, but everyone dreams that one when they're expecting."

"Do they?" Pearl tried to keep herself from snorting.

"Mostly I had these long, involved dreams about logistical stuff—you know, getting on the bus with the wrong change, not having the right stamps for my mail. Boring stuff, but it was terrifying when I was dreaming it. My grandfather was a rabbi, you know, and he told me that dreams are how most people grasp at the divine, even though they don't know it. I mean, the whole

Joseph and Pharaoh thing—it all seems like a riddle, but it's not really, if you know which way to look at it."

Pearl looked at June's white skin; her bathing suit straps cut into her shoulder, and dark pubic hair curled down her thighs and around the edges of her suit. And then June smiled at her from behind the ridiculous sunglasses.

"Don't worry," she said. "It won't last forever. You're almost there." She reached over and put her hand on Pearl's wrist. "Everyone hates being pregnant at the end. And this heat is awful. You're a saint for withstanding it. I couldn't."

Pearl felt the soft pressure of June's hand on her skin. What a funny woman, she thought. She just takes your anger right away from you. The image of Taylor lying on top of June, her head resting on her mother's breasts, twirling her fingers through June's black hair came into Pearl's mind.

"How long are you going to be in the field?" she asked.

"I don't know," June said. "Till we're done, I guess."

"If you ever want to come out, you know, for a rest, you're welcome here," Pearl said smiling. But then she felt June withdraw. Why was that the wrong thing to say? June pulled her hand away.

"Oh, yes," she said and looked over at her daughter, who was sitting in the pool. "I don't think I'll need to do that."

They sat there together, not talking, while Pearl brooded over their conversation. June and Taylor had played the same rude trick on her—they waited for her to be friendly and then acted like she was distasteful. They deserve what they get, she thought. She fell asleep after a while and dreamed of June clearing the fallen frangipani blossoms out of the pool. When she woke up, the mother and daughter weren't there, and she watched the sun set over Port Moresby by herself.

...

Later that evening Pearl went to the *haus was was* with Lidini to fold the laundry. They heard the low murmuring sounds of Peter talking to his wife in the guest room. Lidini stood expressionless while Pearl leaned against the wall and listened.

Baby, Peter was saying, come on, don't worry. We'll be fine.

Pearl pulled away from the wall with Lidini's gaze on her. She was disheartened: this was not what she thought the Campbells would say to each other when they were alone. Their muffled voices kept coming through the wall, and soon the distinct sound of June weeping wrapped itself around Pearl and Lidini, mingling with the smell of Lux and clean, sun-dried cotton in the evening humidity.

Pearl began to fold Steve's shirts and then her own underwear. Lidini matched socks, smoothing and then carefully rounding them into balls the way Pearl had taught her. Pearl imagined Peter holding his wife's head in his lap and stroking her hair as she cried. For a moment she considered walking in and reassuring June, telling her about all the women she knew who had come out of the field unscathed. But then she decided that she didn't want to see her at all, she didn't even want to have dinner with the Campbells. Australia was too far away when she was with them.

Pearl lay in bed that night and stared at the dark window through the mosquito netting. She rolled onto her side and felt the sweat trickle across her back onto the sheet. She lay there like that, awake, listening to the odd truck drive by and her birds calling into the night, and a dog barking. She felt the baby kicking inside, and she knew her upset was keeping it awake, too. Finally, before dawn, she fell into a thick, dreamless sleep where June and Peter Campbell did not exist.

THREE

Peter woke up in the dark and began to put on his running clothes.

"What are you doing?" June asked him from the bed.

"I'm going for a jog," he said.

"You're what? It's the middle of the night," she said.

"No, it's not. Don't you feel the day coming? It's almost morning."

"I can't believe you," she said. She turned on the bedside lamp and watched Peter lace up his sneakers. "Why don't you just go for a swim? Why can't you just swim a thousand laps before sunup or something."

Peter smiled. "I'll be back soon," he said. "Sorry I woke you."

Peter stood outside the wall that surrounded the McGuires' house and breathed in the dust from the road while he listened to a cock crow. At that moment, he realized that it would be impossible to jog through Port Moresby—he didn't know it at all. He looked across the road at the big, wide houses built up on stilts that Pearl had told him were the homes of Australian government officials and some British and French scientists. He thought the structures looked self-conscious, like immense, strutting versions of the natives' houses he had seen as they drove through the capital.

He leaned back against the stucco and stretched his calf, flexing his toes. He was frightened and then annoyed at himself: why was it that as soon as something real was in front of him, he couldn't do it? He couldn't even go for a run. This was everything wrong with him, he decided. This was how it would always be in his life—he could only ever hover in the doorway, peering in. What in the dark morning streets of Port Moresby was worse than this hesitation? He bent over and bounced his fingers along the top of his running shoes. He imagined going back to the bedroom, back to June, and then he closed his eyes and felt the defeat of slipping into the swimming pool, floating with his shorts and sneakers still on. I don't want to be like her, he thought.

Another cock, farther away, let out a limp yodel, and the noise struck Peter as comical. All right, you coward, he thought. Let's just go. He began to run, past the big houses, slowly, careful of his knees. As he moved down the hill, the fences around the houses got taller, and then he was passing empty lots, strewn with garbage and abandoned cement blocks until the road bottomed into a V.

A group of New Guinean men standing around a pickup truck watched Peter appear on the dark road. Brown glass bottles of South Pacific lager were scattered in front of them, and three men who were squatting in a circle playing cards looked up at him. As Peter went past them, a teenage boy who was sitting inside the truck's cab called out to him. The boy opened the door, stumbled onto the road, and began to run after him.

The New Guinean trotted behind him and spoke a rapid Pisin that Peter could not understand. Peter quickened his pace and blew short, hard breaths—hah hah hah—into the air, trying to show that he wasn't scared and didn't want to talk, either. The smell of beer and cigarettes and musky sweat was strong from the boy. He spoke faster and louder and then reached out and ran his fingers along Peter's arm.

"Harim, masta, harim," he said.

The boy's touch scared him. Peter looked at the boy and saw how his eyes were bloodshot and his lips and gums were red from chewing betel nut. This is it, he thought, and he waited for the blow that would trip him to the ground. A truck drove past them honking, and the boy, who was breathing hard now, stopped running and laughed and then yelled after Peter as he sprinted away.

He turned off the airport road, away from the water, and headed in toward town. A few people were gathered outside of the main post office and stared as he jogged past them. Peter wondered if they spent the whole night milling in front of the building. Their attention made him self-conscious, and he looked straight ahead, watching their movements in the half dark out of the corner of his eye.

The sun began to heat the layer of moisture that covered the buildings and dry hillsides. Peter turned left and ran through a row of shabby houses, trying to avoid the discarded candy bar wrappers, chicken shit, and broken glass beer bottles that covered the ground. As the light became stronger, he could see where he was, and he panicked, worrying that nothing was familiar. He expected this path to take him to the coast road after his turnoff. He watched his sneakers slap the ground to distract himself from the frightening thought that he couldn't run for too long in the sun.

Then he recognized a turn that Pearl had made one afternoon after she picked him up. Oh, he thought, discouraged, I really am far away from the house. A few trucks drove past him. After another half hour of running, the blood in his face and the sweat dripping into his mouth crowded out the scared feeling, and he started to enjoy the run. He felt how his lungs were full of the hot air and his legs were pumping a strong, even pace on the dusty, dirt-packed road. Port Moresby was so ugly, but it was exciting then. He wished that he had stopped and talked to the teenager who had followed him. It seemed like a missed opportunity.

The road curved, and Peter quickened his pace as he ran up the hill. His heart was beating hard, and as he leaned into the incline that led up to the McGuires', he wished that June weren't with him. He wished that he were alone and that he was going to bring this all back to her. Everything would be real if she weren't there, so close and greedy for the details of his life. It had always been like this between them—she needed to see the people he worked with, taste the food off his plate, read the research papers he handed in, until he had become secretive of even the most mundane content of his days.

But then his brain was beset by memories of his wife in Boston before they left, buying Abercrombie & Fitch clothes, packing through the night, and shyly showing him the books of poetry and short stories that she had bought. I got them for your mind, she said, so you can restore your creative juices in the field. And there it was—even her generosity felt aggressive. She had so much more money now that her father had died than she did when he first met her, and it had made her rigid and bossy.

The tropical sun was in its full glory, enormous in the sky, pouring white, flat heat into every crevice in the landscape. Peter had a vision of blisters forming on his face. He dropped to a walk and passed the McGuires' house at the next turn. He glanced up the road at the houses and plants and cement-block fences that Pearl had pointed out to him on their morning drives to the hospital.

And when he walked around the corner, the vista was astounding—so dry and bland and then the endless dark Pacific only making everything appear hotter. Well, we're here anyway, he thought. Maybe it was good that she was with him. Maybe this was where he would finally find his wife. He looked east and tried to imagine the lush, green Highlands. But all he saw was the road continuing past the assistant district commissioner's yellow house and a koi dog, hot in the morning sun, lying in the dust looking back at him.

FOUR

The Campbells met patrol officer Leo Hugh-Jones at the head of the Highlands coffee road in Lufa. It was cold and dark in the pre-dawn, and Hugh-Jones said a distracted, quick hello, tossed their luggage to a carrier, and then returned to his preparations. Peter watched the patrol officer, cloaked in his khaki canvas uniform and bush hat, walk back and forth along the line of tired-looking, muscular men with his two Wagi sergeants, uttering quick, clipped Pisin words, checking the sides of the aluminum boxes to make sure they were locked and then that they were lashed securely to the carrying poles.

Peter glanced at June and saw that she was sleepy and anxious and stroking Taylor's hair while she held the girl against her legs. Her breath was white against the darkened air, and it was comforting to see her familiar features. He glanced at two carriers, wearing torn, dirty T-shirts and shorts, who were smoking and talking, squatting on the ground with their toes curled, grasping the ground beneath them. And then Hugh-Jones's voice was clear from far down the road.

"Hapim kago!" he shouted.

Peter and June looked at each other and smiled at the ridiculous-sounding Pisin words. And then the carriers in front of them stood up and lifted the boxes, nestling the poles in the crooks of their necks on worn pieces of cloth.

"Trowim way lek!" Hugh-Jones bellowed, and his voice was full of encouragement and authority.

Peter felt goose bumps on his arms and he reached over and touched June's shoulder.

"Here we go," he whispered, and she smiled at him.

The line of men began to move, and Taylor, who had seemed as though she were asleep, started to cry. She was wearing a white shirt that was printed with red anchors, blue shorts, and big, yellow rubber boots that went up over her knees. He saw her in Boston then, standing on the sidewalk in front of their apartment, waiting for him to lock the door and walk her to school.

"Funny bunny," he said. "Come here."

He picked her up and she was warm. He kissed her hair and held her, waving away the man Hugh-Jones had hired to carry her. June walked at his side, and the three of them were silent as the dark dawn ebbed into gray morning and the fog burned off the hills revealing expanses of purple sweet potato fields at the side of the road. The carriers in front of them marched in a funny off-rhythm, and their strong legs splattered with gray mud looked beautiful to Peter. He was happy like that, and he put his daughter down reluctantly when, at the first real light of morning, the patrol stopped for a break.

. . .

As they got farther south the road narrowed, hacked away, Hugh-Jones said, by the torrential rainy season rains.

"The *kanakas* work like demons in the dry season," he told them when he dropped back and walked with the Campbells, "shoveling, cutting roots and rocks out, making a road wide enough for a coffee truck, and then the rainy season comes and washes all that hard work away."

"It's like Sisyphus," Peter said, smiling.

"The whole bloody country's like Sisyphus," Hugh-Jones said and laughed and walked back up along the line of men to the head of the patrol.

At times the road narrowed into a path of less than two feet, and the carriers had to maneuver their heavy boxes slowly, clamping their bare feet into the slippery, moist earth. Then gradually steep mountains covered in green rain forest emerged on the horizon, and the air became cool and pure tasting. June and Peter walked behind the carrier who had Taylor seated on his shoulders.

Peter was elated: the walking rhythm, the ceaseless pat-pat of the carriers' feet on the earth, the bird calls, and the mountains around them made him feel as though he were only his physical senses—he had no thoughts, he just saw and smelled and heard this world until he felt dizzy with it and had to stop and have some warm Tang from his hip canteen.

He lifted Taylor off the carrier and put her on his own shoulders. When she wanted to walk, he held her hand and told her the story of the Sirens, of Kalypso, of Nausicaa, and finally of Odysseus outwitting the Cyclops. June laughed at his giddiness, at his strange energy, and he could see that she was nervous from him and the place and the quick-slow pace of Hugh-Jones and his carriers.

It began to rain—hard, enveloping rain that poured from the sky with breathtaking force. The ground ran beneath them, rocks and branches flowing past their feet forming rivulets in the clay road.

The rain felt ecstatic to Peter; it filled his eyes and mouth and ears so that he could not hear June when she shouted to him. Hugh-Jones walked down to them and said something, which Peter could not understand, either. But he nodded and smiled anyway and pulled Taylor to him and put his wide-brimmed hat on her head so that the raindrops would not smash onto her face.

The patrol kept going, the carriers slipping, pushed back by the force of thick, dark rain. The rain paused, and the air was suddenly quiet, full of moisture and the overwhelming wet smell of dirt and trees and plants. It was just drizzling then—slow, even raindrops splashing them as the day began to slip away. Thunder started, its loud echo clapping through the valley.

"My god," June said, "is this a monsoon or something?"

"It's just rain," Peter said. "It's just the tropics."

He watched Taylor trudging up the road a few feet in front of them.

"She's so good," he said. "Look at her."

But he didn't think she was being good, really. It was just that she looked exactly right in this landscape—her smallness, her strong pace, the mud on her boots, the way she looked around her, stopping to touch the orchids on the side of the road—she belongs here, he thought.

As they walked through the late afternoon rain, thunder continued to roll through the valley. Lightning began, snapping at the ground in angry white forks, following them, weaving between the carriers' legs and then nipping at June's feet.

"June, stand still!" Hugh-Jones roared at her from the front of the patrol. "It's nothing, it's not like the lightning you're used to—it will go away."

June stood while the lightning snapped a few feet from her and then seemingly disappeared, only to emerge in the distance, lighting up a mountain ridge a thousand feet beyond them. She pulled off her bandanna and laughed, and Peter could see how her dark hair was wet and pressed against her scalp and how the silver fillings in her molars were black in the afternoon light. He knew that she was exhausted and uncomfortable and that her laughter was nervous, but it was for him, too, to show him that she was okay.

"June," he said slowly, gently, "we're almost there."

She looked at him and stopped laughing.

"Do you think you could kiss me, Peter?" she asked.

Her question seemed tangled up in the sadness of the fading light. He glimpsed, for a moment, how much she didn't say to him, how much she felt, and it was unbearable. He was gloomy then and sorry for her. She was lovely, pretty in her dirty, wet, expensive Abercrombie & Fitch and her white white skin. He walked over to her and kissed her wide, soft lips, tasting her sour breath and the sweat and skin smell of her. And when Peter pulled away, he looked at the mountain behind his wife and saw clouds, dense and dark like smoke, clinging to the tree line, bleeding slowly into the deep forest.

...

On the third day the patrol climbed into Abini village.

"Here's where I'd stay if I had to be out here all the time," Hugh-Jones said to Peter and June, nodding out at the amphitheater of rain forest–covered mountains that was visible from the main road. The village's hamlets, occupied by different clans of the same tribe, were dispersed along the mountainside, he explained, as the Campbells followed him up a narrow path that was flanked by sharp-leafed, wild sugar cane plants and smelled of heat and pig excrement. They stared at rough-hewed pig fences that encircled groups of bamboo huts that were roofed in smoke-blackened thatch. A group of villagers, mostly young men and children, followed them as they trekked up the mountain incline to the patrol officer's hut, which was built, in Highlands fashion, at the highest, outermost part of the settlement. The villagers were gawking at Taylor, giggling when she looked at them, shouting and whooping if she said something to her parents or cried in frustration.

The four of them dropped their gear in the hut and shared a Cadbury bar behind the closed door. Then Hugh-Jones led them back down to the main part of the village and stood with them on a bridge over the enormous Abini river, which, he said, flowed from the top of Mt. Abini and crashed through the rain forest over boulders and rocks and moss-covered tree stumps.

"No fish, though," Hugh-Jones said, staring at it wistfully. "Too bloody cold."

The patrol officer went off with his Wagi sergeants to set up a desk at the Church of Christ mission to hear complaints and register births and deaths in the census book. The Campbells, accompanied by a group of twenty staring, giggling villagers, walked back to the hut, past the hamlets that lined the path, and rushed inside the cramped space with relief. They listened to the people outside the hut speaking the odd, stop-and-start vowel sounds of the Abini language until the afternoon rain started and they left.

June put a kettle on the propane stove and boiled water. She made Earl Grey in Hugh-Jones's carefully packed Spode teapot, poured it into cups, and then spooned in powdered milk, stirring until the white grains dissolved. Peter opened the hut's door, and the three of them sat on his cot and watched the rain, drinking their tea, while immense clouds of thin steam rose from the mountainsides and sheets of water fell from the sky, pounding Mt. Philip and the Abini valley.

That night a marsupial rat fell from the rafters onto Taylor's cot and scrambled over her sleeping bag, across her face, and then leaped onto the wall and crawled back into the thatch. The child began to scream and then, hysterical with her fear, started to hyperventilate.

June screamed, "Oh, my god, oh, my god!" and grabbed Taylor out of her sleeping bag. The girl turned red and passed out, and June began yelling at Peter to help. But by the time Peter rushed over, Taylor had regained consciousness, sobbing and hiccuping. She hid her face in her mother's chest, and June kissed the top of her head and rocked her back and forth, while Peter sat crouched at the cot, running his hand along her back.

"It's not like a real rat, sweetheart," Hugh-Jones said to the inconsolable girl. "It's an opossum. It's like a hamster or a gerbil, don't you like those?"

But Taylor only cried harder and slipped her hands inside her mother's shirt and hugged her.

"It'll be hard out here," Hugh-Jones said, jerking his thumb at Taylor and looking at Peter.

"Yes," Peter said.

"How long're you here for, mate?"

"I don't know," Peter said and stood up. "As long as it takes to collect the data—maybe six months, or a year."

"Not too long, then, that's good," the patrol officer said. "What're you looking for?"

"Looking for?" Peter repeated, smiling.

"Yeah, isn't it that you medical researchers are always looking for a disease or a cure or a bug or something?"

"Oh," Peter said. "I'm looking for a parasite, miculla, in the population and how it corresponds to the morb—to the age people are when they die."

Hugh-Jones nodded, and Peter was embarrassed. His research sounded silly and small to his own ears. He shook his head, avoiding the Australian's regard of him.

June was still holding Taylor, rocking her back and forth, running her fingers through the girl's soft, fine hair. The Campbells' belongings were scattered around the hut; their bags lay open, spilling clothes, Taylor's coloring books and dolls, pill bottles, and shoes onto the floor. June had put two plastic buckets filled with cooling water she had boiled and salinated next to the door. Peter's eyes settled on Hugh-Jones's few possessions that were folded neatly under his cot.

A Coleman lamp hung on a nail in the door frame and threw an uneven yellow light on the hut's interior. Peter could feel how his conversation with Hugh-Jones lingered between the four of them. He knew that Hugh-Jones didn't like him, but he didn't want to think about it or figure out the meaning of their strange, awkward interchange.

They went to sleep, the four of them, at almost the same moment, as if none wanted to be awake alone in the uncomfortable, too small space. Peter dreamed vividly that night of a fishing trip he had taken with his father at the summer house when he was a boy, a little older than Taylor. He had sat in their old, painted-red rowboat and watched his father smoke cigarette after cigarette, lighting one off the burning butt of another.

In his dream he became aware that he was there, in New Guinea, in the patrol officer's hut. He was disturbed by this memory playing so clearly in his mind's eye—wasn't his dream getting it wrong? Hadn't the two of them spoken on that trip? His father must have said something to him. Peter saw the image of himself as a little boy row the boat back to the lakeshore. He saw his own face full of yearning, waiting for his father to stop smoking and say something to him.

...

It began every morning early, when a group of children arrived outside the hut and woke the Campbells up with their hushed, giggling voices. When Taylor emerged from the hut, she was surrounded by cooing and laughing children and old women who touched her skin and then yelped. They felt her hair or pinched the back of her legs, crowding around, staring and smiling until she screamed and burst into tears. June would push through the crowd then and walk Taylor to the outhouse, trying to shield her from their prying fingers and eyes.

Taylor could not bear to walk through the village or go with her father to the house site because of the crowd that would gather and touch her. June stayed with her and read her fairy tales or sat on her cot, in the stuffy, lightless hut while the girl colored and the two of them ate melted Cadbury bars and drank Tang. They realized soon that the people who waited outside the hut had begun to poke holes through the woven bamboo wall and stare at them, and when Taylor saw the disembodied brown eyes peering at her, she began to scream and weep and then lay face down on her cot, trying to hide from the Abini villagers' never-ending gaze.

"I hate this, Mommy," she sobbed.

"I know, sweetie pie," June said, heartbroken, watching Taylor, avoiding the eyes and the cluck-clucking sounds from outside the hut. "It's disgusting."

"I want to go back to Boston," she said. "I want to go home."

"I know," June said. "This is too awful."

"This has got to stop, Peter," June said when he arrived back at the hut for lunch. "We're in jail. We're the fucking monkeys at the zoo."

"Jesus, June," Peter said, "I feel terrible. But this is going to calm down—we just have to give them time to get over the novelty of Taylor."

"Yes," she said, "and if they don't, I'm walking out of here with her when Hugh-Jones gets back."

"Oh, June," Peter said. "Come on. You aren't going to do that."

He looked at her and wondered if this was how it would be between them the entire time they were in the field. He understood that she was scared, that this country overwhelmed her, and that she was uncomfortable and disconnected from herself. He wanted to reach out and hold her—he was so excited by this place he almost felt as if his soul had slipped into another body. He wished that she was there with him then, instead of being so afraid.

What would he do if she really left? He had a wild, angry thought of throwing himself on the Abini people's mercy and eating their food and living like them, in one of their small thatch-roof huts. But Peter understood that the villagers expected him to have money. Money and cargo were part of whiteness; he knew it because he had been told it, and he knew it because he had felt it already. The kina bills that he had handed out at the beginning of the house building were crucial to his relationship with them. There was no other truth—he needed June's money. He couldn't stay in Abini without it, and he looked at her then—her flushed cheeks, her dark, incensed expression. He saw the two of them sitting in the cramped hut with the same distance and clarity as he had seen the image of fishing with his father in his dream. How was it, he wondered, that this was his life?

...

At the end of the first week June and Taylor burst from the hut and walked down to the house site, the two of them in an unsmiling fury at the villagers who surrounded them. The site was cut from a wild sugar cane field off the main road and above a leg of the roaring Abini river. Mt. Philip stood close by, its rocky peak jutting from the rain forest, and Mt. Abini was in the distance, surrounded by cloud. A tiny stream ran through the property and would run under the house, Peter explained, so that it would catch their dish and bath water and carry it to the river below.

Peter picked Taylor up and put her on his shoulders and walked around the site with June, nervous and smiling. Six village men were sitting cross-legged, pounding bamboo stalks against thick pieces of wood with rocks, creating long, thin strands. Four other men wove the bamboo strands into wide, green, patterned sheets that would become the house's walls and floor. A team of three men was pounding wide posts into the ground with stone-head mallets, measuring the distance with a long stick of wild sugar cane.

"Here," Peter said, grinning as he stood on top of cut grass in the midst of the workers. "This is our front room, and this here is the kitchen."

He showed June where the bedroom and storeroom and shower stall and his office would be. They walked to the back of the property, and he pointed to the tree stump that marked the outhouse's spot and beyond, a burnt patch of ground for their garden. He was excited then, and he clapped one of the village men on the back.

"Oh," June said, "I am looking forward to this house. I can't stand that hut anymore." She pulled a pack of Marlboros out of her pocket and began to smoke. She stood there, staring out past the working men.

"What a view," she said.

Peter laughed and watched his wife as she surveyed the space, taking in the dark green mountains in the distance, the intense blue of the sky, the clouds perfect and still against the sun.

One of the men shouted, and then four women emerged from the poinsettia bushes that framed the path, sweating and smiling, supporting enormous bulks of green thatch with their backs, their low breasts swaying. They saw June and called to her, waving their hands—*"ay, ay, ay."* June nodded shyly and watched as the men lifted the heavy loads of grass thatch from their backs.

When the women finished unbundling themselves, they came over to June, laughing and smiling. Peter was still carrying Taylor on his shoulders, and he saw them take the cigarette from his wife's mouth and puff on it and then hold her hand and stroke her dark hair. June looked startled, but then she smiled as they made her sit down with them, and they sat there, talking to her in Abini, laughing good-naturedly at each other. They sang to her a funny, tuneless song and rubbed her inner arms, tracing the thick blue veins under her skin.

One of the women ran down to the poinsettia bushes and picked the red leaf-flowers, wiping the milky sap off on her thighs. She wove the poinsettia into a crown and placed it on June's head. The four women kept singing and laughing and speaking to her, and then Peter saw that his wife had begun to cry, smiling at the Abini women who sat with her, nodding as they cooed and wiped away her tears.

. . .

Peter woke up uneasy. He lay in his cot, listening, and realized that it was the silence that had disturbed him out of sleep. The now familiar morning greeting of whispers, giggles, and brushes against the hut's wall was missing: the air was quiet, punctuated only by the wind in the pandanas trees and a high-pitched ka-caw ka-caw in the distance.

"June," he said, rolling onto his side. "Wake up."

"Mmm," she said. "What?"

He shook her arm.

"June," he said. "There's no one here."

She opened her eyes and said, "I don't believe it."

Peter opened the door, and only the Highlands day was outside: the bright blue sky, the tree line, a thatch roof in a distant hamlet seeping smoke into the air.

"How weird," she said and sat up in bed.

They got up then, the three of them, and quietly began their morning routine: Peter walked Taylor to the outhouse, June boiled porridge and a kettle for the instant coffee, Peter brushed his teeth with salinated water and spat into the narrow flood gutter that ringed the hut.

By mid-morning, sounds of the uninterrupted day—a beetle screaming across the valley, the wind ruffling the roof thatch, a rooster crowing halfheartedly—engulfed Peter. His mind began to race. Why was no one there? Had he done something wrong in the negotiations over the house building? Had they offended the villagers by keeping Taylor hidden in the hut all day? He hated that he could not really speak or understand Pisin. Pisin still sounded foolish, like baby talk to him, but he knew that it was a real language, full of nuance.

June and Taylor played cards, spreading the deck over the slippery nylon surface of June's sleeping bag. When had Hugh-Jones said he was walking back? Peter couldn't remember anymore.

"What's the date, June?" he asked her.

"The date?" she repeated. "I don't know—maybe the 15th or the 16th. Why?"

When he didn't answer, she said, "Peter, are you going to go down to the house site?"

"Yes," he said. "I think I will."

"I see," she said. "That's probably a good idea."

Taylor looked up at him and smiled. Of course, he thought, the girl is only relieved that the crowd isn't here, that she can play gin rummy unobserved with the beautiful day flowing into the hut, flushing her in cool mountain air. Peter smiled at his daughter.

"I think I'll stay till lunch," he said.

He rooted through his duffel bag and found his notebook. He sat next to June and flattened the book out on his lap and half listened to the sweet noise of his wife and daughter laughing and talking over their card game. The Abini are malnourished, he wrote. Almost all the children have distended bellies, ring worms, rickets, and tropical ulcers. He sketched Mt. Philip, drawing it in long, black, ink strokes, and then he drew the hut and Taylor sitting on the cot, hunched over her cards.

At noon June opened a tin of tuna fish and spooned it onto saltines, and they drank warm Tang and sucked on Callard & Bowser butterscotches for dessert.

"Okay," he said, "here I go."

He saw how June and Taylor were sleepy and slow as they washed the plastic plates in the bucket by the door. June had unpacked *Tropic of Cancer,* and Peter looked at the book lying in the folds of her sleeping bag and the bright colors of the dust jacket dissolved in the too white daylight. They waved to him as he walked away and called "bye-bye." Peter heard Taylor giggling as he started down the path, but soon the only sounds were the buzz of cicadas and the heavy thump-thump of his hiking boots. Two small brown birds flew in front of him, their wings fluttering as they chased each other into the wild sugar cane field.

The first hamlet he passed was silent, the huts boarded up. Two fat pigs dozing under the shade of a scraggly coffee tree looked up at him dispassionately and grunted. Soon after he passed the hamlet, he heard someone calling out a sing-song sentence in Abini, but the voice was fleeting, barely perceptible in the endless expanse of mountain and valley. A small boy, naked except for a ratty string tied around his belly stood at the edge of the path smiling at him.

"Apinoon, masta," the boy said.

"Apinoon," Peter said, searching for Pisin words. *"Man i go we?"* he asked finally.

Instead of answering, the boy smiled and took Peter's hand. The boy probably didn't know Pisin, Peter thought. Hugh-Jones had told them that this far away from Goroka only young men who had ventured into the rest of New Guinea would know Pisin.

"Yu kam," the child said, tugging on Peter's arm and nodding down the path. *"Mi bai sowim yu."*

The boy held on to Peter's hand, smiling up at him and then scratching at the tropical ulcers on his shins. Peter was wary; he wanted to shake free of this child's insistent grip and go back to June and Taylor. He stopped and wiped his shirtsleeve against his sweating forehead. His nose and lips were burning in the intense equatorial sunlight.

"*Yu kam,*" the boy repeated, tugging on his hand.

The two of them followed the path as it widened and then emptied onto the road near the Campbells' house site. But the boy kept pulling him along the road, pointing to an unfamiliar path that led up a hill to a tanket-plant fence. When they got up the incline, Peter saw that the boy had brought him to a hamlet that was milling with what looked like hundreds of people. A rectangular house flanked by banana trees stood at the far end, and several smoke-darkened huts dotted the rest of the space. A few villagers from the throng looked at him with surprised expressions, smiled, and uttered, "*Apinoon, masta.*"

As he climbed over the tanket fence, he saw a line of cooked pigs, spread in the midst of the villagers. He calculated that there were thirty dead animals lined up on the ground (most of them mature but a few small, suckling ones, too), split open from their snouts to their anuses. Their sliced-open bodies revealed tangled pink intestines, yellow fat, and cooked white muscle. The pigs had been roasted in a fire; their skin was black, their sooty hairs dark against the orange earth.

An older man in a canvas hat and loincloth was standing over one of the pigs shouting a long stream of Abini words, gesticulating into the air. Flies swarmed over the split pigs. Peter began calculating the protein, the bacteria, the fat, and the parasites of this feast. Won't they all get trichinosis? he wondered, or are they inured to it from exposure? He looked around the hamlet for outhouses—he knew that the Australians had forced most of the Highlands' villages to dig toilets in the 1960s, but he couldn't see any.

Two young men began cutting up the pigs with sharp Okapi knives, slicing thick squares of pork and then laying them out on banana-leaf plates. A man whom Peter recognized from the house building came up to him.

"*Apinoon,*" he said smiling, "*mipela kai kai pik.*" We're eating pigs.

"Yes," Peter said, wondering what he meant. Was this sort of pig kill a regular occurrence or a ritual? Was everyone in the whole village there, all eating from the same batch of pigs? He wished that he could express himself, and he stood there, frustrated, staring at the man's lips and gums and teeth that were dyed deep red from betel nut.

"*Yu laik kai kai?*" the man asked him.

Is that what they all thought? That he was waiting for a piece of pork? Peter was mortified, worried that he would be handed a slice of the disease-ridden, undercooked meat and be expected to eat it right in front of them.

He shook his head. "*Nogat,*" he said.

The man smiled and shrugged his shoulders and walked over to stand in line for his portion of the meat. Peter stood watching women and children and men eat, feasting on the greasy cooked pig, smiling and talking. He was shy to be there, uninvited and barely able to communicate, but he could not leave. He was riveted by them as they avidly consumed flesh that he knew was teeming with microbes, parasites, fecal matter, and bacteria.

The light was fading quickly, and once all the pigs were divided up and distributed, the villagers began to go inside their huts. A few people waved at him, looking at him, polite but curious. By the time the dark came, Peter was alone, standing, listening to the muted sounds coming through the huts of fires crackling and people talking and singing in Abini.

He walked out of the hamlet slowly, carefully climbing over the tanket fence and navigating his way to the wide, main road. As he walked, images of the cooked, butchered pigs, and New Guineans stuffing their mouths with the greasy pink meat, and the mountains in the full afternoon sunlight beset his mind.

He retraced his steps along the road and then up the mountain path, stumbling in the dark, trying to use the slight illumination of the half moon to find his way. He was breathing hard, pumping his legs and arms, listening to the scurry of nocturnal animals and birds in the forest around him. Wild sugar cane leaves brushed his arm, and he thought of what he would write in his notebook. The place seemed rich and full of secrets. He felt as though he had been allowed a look at the essence of the place.

Yellow light shone through the cracks in the hut's bamboo wall. He imagined June lighting the Coleman, pumping the bag, pushing her hair behind her ear, kissing Taylor's cheek. When he opened the door, his wife was lying on her cot, reading. She smiled at him.

"We missed you, Dr. Livingston," she said.

Taylor was asleep, dressed in her pink flannel pajamas.

"Oh, June," he said. "You can't believe where we are."

He looked down at his sleeping daughter, and he wanted to touch her; he wanted her to feel this place with him. He lifted her out of the cot, and she woke up and looked at him sleepily.

"What are you doing, Peter?" June asked, laughing.

He walked outside the hut with Taylor in his arms and pointed to the mass of stars in the equatorial night sky. June came and stood next to him. A bat flew by them, whooshing through the cool mountain air. He wanted to say something to the two of them, but he didn't know what it was yet.

So Peter stood like that, holding his child, letting his heart beat onto her skin, feeling how the whole place was throbbing with night animals and birds and the dense net of stars in the Southern Hemisphere's sky, until she said, "I'm cold, Daddy," and he kissed her and walked back into the hut.

part two

A young woman from Ogekapa village bumped her foot on her way home from the kitchen garden. She cried out, but her mother and brother were far ahead, past the overgrown arbor of coffee trees on the other side of the re-growth forest, and did not hear her. The girl sat on a stone watching as bright red blood spilled from her toe onto the moss and wet earth of the forest floor.

When it got dark and the rain started, she made a shelter and de-cided to wait for her mother to come back in the morning. But her mother never came, and she stayed in the forest for many days, bleeding from her foot, hunting kapul, eating tani mushrooms and roasted beetles, and sleep-ing at night in the curve of a tree hollow.

When people in Ogekapa asked her mother where her daughter was, she shook her head and said maybe the girl had gone to visit cousins in

Abini. But the young woman was in the forest near her mother's garden. Sometimes she would hear her mother's and brother's voices echo through the tree canopy, and she would call out to them, but she only sounded like a faraway, hungry bird to them. She wept then, full of loneliness.

Late in the day the young woman would stumble up to the edge of the Ogekapa garden and eat from the pile of sweet potatoes, taro, cut sugar cane, and green kumu that her mother left in a pile near the pig fence. And the next time her mother came to the gardens, she would pick up the gnawed ends of sweet potato tubers, shake her head, and say, "Ay, the rats are very bad, stealing all our food."

FIVE

After four months in the field, *tok ples* words flowed from Taylor's mouth as smoothly as the white round worms Peter pulled out of her anus after she swallowed a dose of Mebendazole. It was only when she spoke with her parents that she stuttered and frowned, full of the effort of answering them in English.

June worried that her daughter spoke English so weakly, dropping words and confusing verb tenses. At night, as she poured hot water from a kettle into the square fiberglass bathtub, she told Taylor Mother Goose tales, nodding as she talked and filling the house's narrow rooms with nonsense rhymes and baby talk endearments. June soaked a washcloth in Phisoderm and ran it along Taylor's body, tracing her belly and armpits and even the soles of her feet and the tender skin between her toes, all the while naming their friends in Boston by first and last name, Taylor's nursery school teachers, and the streets they lived near.

In the Coleman's yellow light June could see how the disinfectant she stirred into the bathwater inflamed the scratches and rashes on Taylor's body, making a red zigzag pattern across her thighs and shins. And when June was done scrubbing her, Taylor pulled the stopper from the tub and the bathwater, dirty with her sloughed skin and the orange earth that stuck to her legs and arms, drained beneath the house, making a slapping noise as it hit the ground.

Taylor stood in the empty tub, and June patted Calamine onto her and then brushed her daughter's hair back from her forehead. She looked tidy then and pink as she stepped naked from the tub and walked to her room, making the woven-bamboo floor crackle under her bare feet. June followed her and dug out the dirt that clung to the soft flesh under Taylor's fingernails with a wood toothpick. Then she took her daughter's small hands in hers and slowly sucked on her fingers, running her tongue along the girl's cuticles and under her nail beds until she could no longer taste the chemical disinfectant or the gritty earth.

...

During their early days in the field, when the Campbells had moved out of the patrol officer's hut into their own house, Taylor stayed close to her parents while they worked. She clutched her father's legs while he set up his tripod and photographed the scabies blisters that twisted around a boy's shins or the distended, goitered neck of an old woman with the click hiss of the Nikon's shutters. June wrote down the names of the villagers that her husband photographed and tried to map their blood relationships on Peter's neat, black-inked kinship charts. Taylor cried, irritated by the intense sunlight that burned her skin and the smell of sweat and smoke and human excrement that filled the hamlets.

Old women and children continued crowding around Taylor, surrounding her with the musky odor that came from their armpits and beneath their bark–string skirts. And it was especially bad when June and Peter took her to a new hamlet, where she had never been seen up close: the people reached out and rubbed her skin and stroked her hair, and then clucked their tongues when she shouted "Go 'way" and began sobbing. But the villagers only knelt closer to her and wiped up her tears with a piece of dried pandanas leaf and licked it.

"Peter," June said when Taylor was crying, "pick her up."

Peter hoisted his weeping daughter over his head and sat her on his shoulders. She lay her cheek on her father's hair and wrapped her arms around his neck and looked off into the distance at Mt. Abini and the sky that stretched over the mountains, blue and full of a too close sun.

But by their third month in the field, Taylor no longer stayed with her parents while they worked. After they ate breakfast June and Peter left her, carrying their cameras, baby scales, and Styrofoam nests of syringes and test tubes, hurrying to get ahead of the mid-morning heat that covered the Lido valley.

And when, in the midst of working, June looked up from the scales and asked a villager where the children were, someone would point into the green distance and say, *"Lukim, em istap."* Peter, shielding his eyes against the sun, told June that he could see them, a slowly moving black line among the trees.

Peter had a birder's eye; back in the States he could see owls in the dense pine trees of Acadia Park and a familiar face five city blocks away. His father was a fighter pilot who had dropped bombs across the Pacific and sat in a bunker with Douglas MacArthur. When June looked out at the expanse of green forest, she thought about Peter's father, with his skinny body and deep-set eyes and the endless Pall Malls he smoked. She liked that Peter and his father saw into the distance. Her husband's keen eyesight and hearing seemed extraordinary to her, and it made her feel safe as she stood with him there in Abini watching the mountains that surrounded them.

...

Gradually, the Campbells developed a routine in the field. They followed the villagers, who woke in the cold blue predawn and were dozing in their huts when equatorial night brought darkness to the day as quickly as a door slamming shut. And in the early evening, when the cicadas were still crying their night warning, June waited for Taylor at the back door of their house. She could see her daughter climb over the tanket fence and then disappear until her dirt-covered face loomed out of the darkness. The girl seemed like a vision then, and sometimes when she appeared so close June started, frightened.

As Taylor walked past her through the door, her legs and shoes encrusted with earth and sticky tree sap streaks on her arms and face, she was full of stories of abandoned pandanas groves lined with the graves of babies. Dead children became spirits, she told Peter and June, and haunted the fast-flowing rivers that gushed out of the mountain's rocky belly. The spirits hid in tree branches, and in the rain forest floor, and in the huge, gray rocks that broke the river's fierce flow, sending spraying arcs into the air, waiting to find a lone child in the forest and kill it.

As the months passed and the rainy season became dry, Taylor went even farther away from the village and her parents' compound with her friends and their mothers, trekking all morning over the Abini mountain range to enormous kitchen gardens. Taylor told her mother about walking for hours in the dense forest and then finally coming into the sunlight and seeing tanket-plant and woodplank fences that looked as though they had risen out of nowhere in the middle of their path. The lashed-together fences encircled steep slopes of sweet potato ivy and uneven rows of maroon sugar cane and pandanas trees with their spiny, spindly leaf tops. She said that the gardens spread wide, reaching farther than she could see and that they were creepily silent after the constant noise of the rain forest, with only the sound of a nearby river or a crying baby to disturb the day. Taylor and her friends lay on the carpet of ivy and dirt and watched the women plant sweet potato and taro, chanting spells and lullabies to the tubers that lay impacted in the soft earth.

...

Then, without any warning, Taylor could speak Abini. June and Peter could not recall a learning period, a month when the girl communicated awkwardly with the villagers. By the time June noticed her daughter speaking the native language, the girl was spitting out long sentences at her friends, laughing with them, and joining in songs and chants, and when June's back was turned to Taylor and her friends, she could barely distinguish her daughter's voice from those of the other children.

...

One afternoon Taylor came back to the compound from the gardens with a woman and her two daughters. The woman, Nari, had brought a net bag full of corn and yellow stub cucumbers and sweet potato to sell to June, and as she walked to the doorway, the three girls crawled under the house.

June took the vegetables and gave the woman a kina coin and a biscuit. The two of them stood there, smiling, awkward together while they listened to their daughters chattering through the bamboo floor. Nari squatted down and began to eat the biscuit, looking around at the cast-iron stove and the spigot that emptied into a deep fiberglass sink. After a while she stood up and smoothed the biscuit crumbs from her bark-string skirt onto the floor. They could hear the click of pebbles hitting each other as the girls played a game.

Nari nodded at June and said: *"Tenk yu, misses."*

"Thank you," June said.

June watched the woman walk out the door and down the steps toward the compound's fence.

"Taylor," she called into the dusk, "come in now." But she knew her daughter would play outside until her friends left. She began to husk Nari's corn, ripping the green skin in quick, jerky movements and then picking silk off the short ears. Peter was typing up notes on the Olivetti, and the even rhythm was clear from the back of the house until one of the girls started to yodel. The girl sang out across the shallow valley, her rich voice sending a series of sing-song questions to a nearby hamlet.

Peter walked into the kitchen and pushed out the window over the sink. The two of them looked at Taylor, who had climbed on top of the boulder at the south end of the compound. She was unmistakable through the blue evening as she stood there with her hands on her hips and her head tilted, concentrating, listening to the response echoing back to her.

"My god," Peter said. "I *thought* that was Taylor."

June nodded her head and stared at her daughter. She could not see Nari, but the woman's daughters were close to Taylor, crouched, squatting on the edge of the boulder, their arms hugging their necks as they looked in the direction of the hamlet.

Peter hurried to the back of the house and got the two-reeled Sony and walked outside, stepping with exaggeratedly careful steps. June watched him set up the tape recorder on the boulder. He held the microphone toward Taylor, and the two girls, nervous to be so close to him, covered their mouths with their hands and giggled. From the kitchen June heard Peter whisper the time and date over the night sounds and the girls' whispers and Taylor's yodeling. And then, as he checked the needle bouncing over the levels, he said: "Taylor, the native."

June clenched her teeth and drew in a long, deep breath. Peter was so clumsy, she thought, and she wanted to call to him, to tell him to stop. Instead, she pulled the window shut and smoothed her hair behind her ears. She put on the kettle for Taylor's bath and started cooking, filling the kitchen with the sound of her knife slapping through carrots onto the chopping board and the smell of onions frying in thick, Australian-export vegetable oil. She tuned Peter's shortwave radio to the BBC World Service and listened to the broadcast and didn't say anything when they came inside the house, shivering from the cold mountain night.

. . .

In those early, dreamlike months in the Highlands June felt that the insistent tropical sun and the rainstorms that raged every afternoon had invaded her being so that she could not think of anything beyond the intense physical reality of Abini. She could not imagine not knowing the intimacy of the place, the wet scent of the earth after the rains and the smell of pig excrement and smoke in a hamlet in the midday sun.

She thought about Pearl McGuire then, and wondered about the baby's birth and if she were still in Australia or if she had come back to the unrelenting heat and humidity of Port Moresby, sweating and miserable with her newborn baby.

June had been almost melancholy when they left Pearl at the Moresby airport and got on the Air Niugini flight to Goroka, the capital of the Eastern Highlands Province. Pearl had said that Goroka was pleasant, easy, and cool, and it was: the Campbells had gone to the British Medical Institute's lab and met with Tony Fitzroy, a Welsh physician and researcher who was a tropical-parasite expert. Peter's doctoral advisor at Harvard had recommended that he meet with both Steve McGuire in Moresby and Fitzroy in Goroka. Peter and June were excited as they shook his hand and looked at him in his white lab coat, so incongruous and familiar that they had laughed from their nerves.

Fitzroy had ushered them into the lab and started lecturing them, describing the symptoms of hookworm, roundworm, whipworm, tapeworm, and pinworm. He told them they would get worms from eating food prepared by a villager, from holding a child close to their mouths, or from walking barefoot on the sun-warmed, tropical earth.

The British lab was filled with brushed-steel double sinks, enormous refrigerators, and squat centrifuges that dotted the back room. As June and Peter sat on tall stools, listening to Fitzroy, they were surrounded by the hum of refrigerators. The smell of fried lard biscuits and magnolia blossoms poured through the louvered windows, diluting the scent of formaldehyde and alcohol that breezed through the rooms.

June was still tired from their trip from the States and the short stay in Port Moresby with Pearl McGuire and the early morning flight into Goroka the day before. As she looked around the lab, it seemed to her like a landscape from a dream and she nodded and tried to concentrate while Fitzroy talked.

"Of course," Fitzroy had said then, "tapeworm is what you really want to avoid. We had a Dutch missionary in Wagi grow one thirty feet long in her gut."

"My god," Peter said, smiling.

"She only had black tea and tapioc root gruel three times a day for months."

"Didn't she starve?" June asked.

"A bit—she did a bit. However, she had the good book for sustenance, and the worm didn't. Eventually, we held a honey-soaked swab at a few of the lady's choice openings, and when the worm poked its head out, we nabbed it. We wrapped it, very slowly, around a stick. It's the way it's been done since King Tut's time.

I've got her worm here in a jar." He traced his palm down a steel refrigerator door.

Peter made a choking noise and waved his hand in mock horror.

"Please," he said, laughing, looking at the refrigerator. "My wife'll turn around and go straight back to Boston."

"Let's have lunch then, shall we?" Fitzroy said, smiling. He gave June Mebendazole tablets in plastic blisters and led them into the lab's outer office to get Taylor, who was sitting on a couch drawing in one of Peter's notebooks. Fitzroy walked them along a smoothed dirt road, pointing out the mountains and the still helicopters that fanned out from the airstrip and then the path that led to the Bird of Paradise.

The hotel's roof restaurant was crowded with Australian officials, medical researchers, and missionaries. The four of them sat under an umbrella, and Fitzroy nodded and waved greetings to different people. They ordered tomato-and-cheese sandwiches and Schweppes that came to the table in short, thick-ridged glass bottles that were beaded with sweat. Fitzroy told them about the Institute's research on tropical ringworm, scabies, cradle cap, trichinosis, and slow-growing viruses that were spread by intestinal worms. He said these viruses invaded nerve tissue and ate the delicate protein that housed neurons. You could tell afflicted people just by the way they walked, he said.

Fitzroy smiled at Peter and told him how much they needed information on the rural population. It seemed to June that Fitzroy had just remembered who they were. She did not like that they were so unimportant, that they faded behind a lunchtime chat about tropical medicine. How many inexperienced researchers had he welcomed to the Eastern Highlands, affirming his connection to their advisors, earning credit with established scientists? Although they were there, in front of him, filled with jet lag and nervous excitement, Fitzroy was not really with them; he was making an exchange with men he had never met, scientists back in Cambridge.

"You've got your work cut out for you," he smiled at them.

"Don't we," June said, and Peter turned to her, surprised at her vehemence.

June continued to watch Fitzroy as she ate lunch. His brown hair was thick and cut close to his scalp and his broad nose was sunburned pink. He made wide curlicue patterns in the air with his fingers while he talked and gave the table a light, careful slap when he laughed. June liked the quick, clipped tones of his British accent there in Goroka. All of a sudden she was glad to hear the immense detail of his work, the endless sorting and categorizing of blood and worms and microscopic bacteria. It reminded her of being in the apartment in Boston and listening to Peter talk about his research and the Harvard labs.

June felt as though she were drifting in a dream. The sun, held back by water-heavy rain clouds, made Goroka feel too bright to her, and she looked off the roof at the banana trees that grew along the road and the low, kunai-covered foothills that surrounded the airstrip. June turned and saw her daughter swinging her legs and eating the potato crisps that had been piled next to her sandwich.

"Taylor," June said, unaware that she was interrupting Fitzroy, "do you love Mommy so much?"

The girl looked up from her plate at her mother and then at Peter and Fitzroy. She put her hands in her lap and smiled at June.

"Yes, Mommy," she said and giggled. The child looked unsure and began to blink and then made a face at her mother.

June laughed and leaned over the table and kissed Taylor's cheek. As she leaned back in her chair, the sun drifted behind a stand of thick clouds. She was relieved, then, by the shade that covered the hotel's roof.

...

At their field site, away from the packed dirt roads and corrugated aluminum houses of Goroka, June dosed the three of them with Mebendazole. And then white worms, eight inches long and thick as a pencil, came out of Taylor. For three days after Taylor swallowed the Mebendazole she got cramping diarrhea and sat in the outhouse with a tin lantern at her feet, crying from the pain in her bowels.

The first time the child was ill from the dose, Peter got Fitzroy on the two-way radio. Fitzroy explained the drug to them, and how the worms were living in Taylor's large intestine, nourished from the protein in her gut. She'll be all right, he told them through the crackle of radio waves that bounced against the Abini mountains.

But Taylor got sick from the Mebendazole every time June gave it to her, and said that the chloroquine they took against malaria made her nauseated and burp up a bitter taste. June gave her spoonfuls of Tiptree jam and squares of Cadbury's to fight the drug's queer aftertaste, but the girl shook her head and pursed her lips from the quinine anyway.

...

And eventually, June found lice in Taylor's hair and began kneading strong-smelling yellow Quell into her scalp during the nightly disinfectant baths. She cut the girl's hair short, trimming the fine strands that grew along the nape of her neck and along her forehead. And it was soon after June found the lice, and she was examining her daughter's body with her fingers, searching her skin and hair for parasites, that she noticed a rash of white, angry-looking hives that speckled the girl's belly, running from below her chest to the tops of her thighs.

"Taylor," she asked, "what is this? When did this start?"

"I don't know," her daughter said and tried to cover her skin with her hands.

June unhooked the Coleman from the nail above the bathtub and brought it down to the floor next to her.

"Taytie," she said, "come over here. Let me see you."

Taylor stayed still, standing in the bathtub. She shook her head no.

"Come on, Taylor," June said, and she was angry then. "Now."

She pulled Taylor toward her and held the Coleman close to her daughter's body. There were dozens of large white bumps that spread out onto her thighs and groin and the bottom of her belly, surrounded by skin that was red and splotchy. June reached out and touched the hives gently, feeling the bumps and ridges with her fingertips. The thought that the bumps were worm larvae embedded in Taylor's thin, delicate skin occurred to her, and she drew her hand back quickly, horrified. She put the lantern down. She felt sick then kneeling on the bamboo floor.

"Doesn't it hurt, sweetheart?" she asked, quietly.

"I don't feel it," Taylor said and shrugged. "It itches."

And while the girl was in front of her, standing naked in the bath with the Coleman on the floor lighting up the scratches and tropical ulcers on her legs and the dirt specks in the bathwater, June felt a flush travel from her groin up to her neck. Something must have happened, she thought. She imagined Taylor away from her, up in the gardens, naked, lying on the worm-filled earth.

"What happened?" she asked. "Did something happen?"

Taylor looked down, away from her mother. The girl was square—her shoulders, her hips, even her legs were square and strong from climbing the mountains and playing all day in the gardens. The bumps on her skin seemed immense, and June wondered when it had started. How many nights had it been obscured in the Coleman's weak light?

"Taylor," she said, "how long has this been on you?"

This rash could not have been on her daughter without her seeing it.

"I don't know, Mommy," Taylor said. She looked up at her mother. "I'm cold. I want to get out."

There it was. Taylor was offering her back the comfortable silence between them. June felt enormously tired; she could see how everything had gone wrong, and she felt sorry for her daughter and guilty, too. I did this, she thought. I made her this closed off from me.

"Taytie," she said, and she heard the anger in her voice, but she could not control it. "You have to tell me when something's wrong with you."

"It's nothing," Taylor began to cry. "I don't even feel it." She stood there crying a low, tearless whine with her chin on her chest.

Taylor got out of the bath, and June covered her in a towel, and then the girl walked past her down the hall into her bedroom. June walked into the kitchen and stood staring at Peter, who was sitting, writing in his journal in careful script next to drawings of flowering trees. He must have heard us, she thought. Why doesn't he just come?

She told Peter what she had found on Taylor.

"Maybe," she said, "you could make a diagnosis."

"June," Peter said, "Jesus, I can't imagine. Maybe it's an allergy or something."

"That's right," she said, furious that he had removed himself. "You're not a doctor."

Peter went into Taylor's room, and as June held the lamp up to the girl, who was still naked from her bath, he saw the hives and the swelling and the redness. He sucked in his breath.

"Christ," he said. "Tay, doesn't this hurt?"

Taylor shook her head again and looked down at her body, gazing at the lumps disinterestedly.

"There's more, Peter, there's more. They're growing!" June shrieked. Her voice sounded absurd and hysterical to her. Taylor began crying again as June pointed to bumps that ran around her daughter's armpits and across her chest in an uneven path.

"Stop it, June," Peter said. "Calm down."

He walked out of Taylor's room and switched on the two-way radio. June listened to him call Goroka, and then she heard Fitzroy talking.

"I don't know what sort of thing it is," Fitzroy said over the radio. "It doesn't sound too good, though. You should bring her to Goroka."

The two men agreed that Fitzroy would go by the Seventh Day Adventists' pilots quarters and get one of them or Mitch Kinsey, an Australian pilot for hire, to fly out to Abini as soon as possible. They would be there in the morning if the clouds didn't block the mountain pass, Fitzroy said.

June sat on the edge of Taylor's cot and watched her daughter put on her pajamas; she watched her button the worn cotton top and then slip on the bottoms. She stood up and pulled back the covers. This is all wrong, she thought. We're too far away from an emergency room for this. An impression of the immense dark, full of rain forest–covered mountains, that they were in the midst of crowded her mind. It was as though they were at the bottom of the ocean. Everything real and familiar was so far away that even the thought of home was distorted. Taylor shouldn't have been allowed to go off and roam with the villagers. She and Peter had made a mistake. She shook her head and then bent down to kiss Taylor and tasted how hot her skin was and the disinfectant from the bath and the tears on her cheeks.

"I don't want to go, Mommy. I want to stay here."

"Taylor," she said, "we have to get you out of the field."

"Please," Taylor said. June heard how scared the child was, and she felt sorry for her.

"I'm coming, too," June said. "You're not going anywhere without me, sweetie."

She took the Coleman off the nail and walked into the kitchen.

"I'll go," June said. "I'll go with her."

Peter nodded his head.

"I want to call my mother, anyway," she said. "And the bank in Boston."

She waited for Peter to hear the upset in her voice and say that he would come with her. June was scared to be without him in New Guinea. She saw how her husband was resisting. He did not want to go with her, and she knew that he was not going to say anything. Was it Taylor? she wondered. Was it that he knew that it was the end? They would have to leave the field now and go back to Boston. She felt how much he did not want to go back to Cambridge and his department. She thought: It's not this place. We could be anywhere, as long as we're far away from home.

"This is real," she said. "This is what it's like here."

"Okay," Peter said.

"Do you think one of us should stay awake and watch Taylor?"

"I don't know," he said. "I don't think so."

She listened to him walk to Taylor's room and soothe her. And then he went out the back door, down the stone-slab steps toward the outhouse.

The water from Taylor's bath was lukewarm when June put her hand in and pulled the stopper. As the tub drained, she pushed the sediment to the side and wiped it up with a sponge. They would leave the field, she thought. She imagined the perfectly packed cardboard boxes in their apartment, filled with folded clothes and moth balls, and the furniture covered in thick plastic sheeting and her arrangements at the bank, so efficient that her checking account in Goroka swelled every month and the car insurance in Boston was taken care of. The fantasy of an early, unexpected return to the States disturbed her. Everything was impossible again just when she had begun to feel comfortable. She would have to argue with Peter; they had agreed they would not stay in New Guinea if it was too hard on the girl.

The fleeting, angry thought that Taylor should not have been so willful—that she shouldn't have roamed so far into the forest and picked up whatever horrifying tropical bug this was flashed through June's mind.

"That is silly," she murmured out loud, and she was embarrassed that she was annoyed with her daughter.

She stood up and walked into the kitchen. She washed her hands and face and brushed her teeth and peered into the little mirror that hung from a nail over the sink. Her skin was freckled from the Abini sun. She brushed her hair back and then ran her fingers through it, feeling for knots.

When June got to the bedroom, Peter was still in his bed. She lay down. Her nose was cold, and she pulled the blankets up around her neck and cupped her hands over her mouth and breathed hot air into them, trying to warm her face. After a while she heard Taylor's breathing, stuffed up from her earlier crying fit, and then Peter's lighter breathing mingling with his daughter's.

June listened to the stream running under the house and the marsupial rats scurrying and burrowing into the thatch roof. As she fell into a shallow sleep, uncomfortable from the chilled air that permeated the woven walls, she wanted to go to her daughter's room, and for a moment she was disoriented and thought she was back in their Boston apartment. She saw the apartment with its white walls and carpeted stairs and tried to wake herself to go to Taylor. She woke up then and knew she was in Abini.

When she did sleep that night, she felt Mt. Abini and Mt. Philip beyond it, wide and heavy, surrounding the hamlets that trickled across the mountain reaches. And in her dreams she watched herself as she slept with Taylor at her side on the road that ran past the compound and then around Beriapi and out of Abini. She was slight and pale in the half-moon light, and she shifted, reaching out to hold her daughter close to her belly and her breasts, trying to get comfortable on the cold Eastern Highlands ground.

As June awoke, she saw the dawn light nudge its way through the cracks in the wall and heard the village roosters crying the morning across the Abini valley. She could not remember sleeping at all during the night. When she looked over at her husband, who slept with one arm dangling off the bed and the blanket stretched over his familiar, long body, she felt the muscles in her chest tighten. Everything she knew was with her.

SIX

June had drunk two cups of coffee at the Lutheran guest house, and she felt the sourness in her mouth and stomach, and as she looked into the fog, she realized how happy she was to be out of the field. Goroka looked nice that morning. The short buildings made from fiberglass and corrugated aluminum sat in back of neat, carefully tended gardens that sported rows of impatiens and sweet peas. June thought of Peter and was annoyed that he was not there with them. She took a pack of Marlboros from her pocket and began to smoke.

She and her daughter walked toward the British Medical Institute's buildings, through the morning that was still as cold as the night before, the roads filled with water-heavy air and filtered sunlight. June wore a denim wrap skirt, an old sweater of Peter's, and red espadrilles that tied around her ankles with wide cloth ribbons. The shoes were impractical for the steep dirt roads, and she slipped as she walked. Taylor was half asleep, carrying a coloring book and *Asterix in Egypt* in her arms.

The British Institute's red brick buildings were flat with narrow, louvered windows and straight-cut paths crisscrossing the grounds. The place felt like a suburban high school to June, modern, ugly, and comforting.

When they got to Fitzroy's lab, he was sitting, drinking Nescafé from a Styrofoam cup. June said good morning, and he smiled awkwardly and offered her a cup of coffee. He walked ahead of them past the centrifuges and the brushed-steel refrigerators to a small room.

"I'm not really set up here," he said.

A black vinyl bench was pushed against the wall close to a sink, and a metal stand covered with syringes, test tubes, and glass slides stood near the door. June leaned against the wall and said, "That's all right, Tony. We thought you could maybe just take a look."

June took the books from Taylor's hand and watched Fitzroy examine her. At first it seemed like he was just giving her a checkup, peering into her eyes, ears, and throat, taking her blood pressure, weighing her. But then Fitzroy drew two tubes of blood and eased the girl's shirt over her head and stood back while she took off her pants. In the lab's artificial light the hives looked much worse than they had in Abini. Fitzroy put on latex gloves and made Taylor stand with her legs apart. He ran his gloves over her chest and armpits, and then he bent down and peered at the rash on her thighs.

He shook his head—"And it doesn't hurt or itch, dear?"

"It itches," Taylor said.

Tony frowned and took a blunt steel scraper and ran it down Taylor's back and then along the inside of her arms. Bright red lines appeared on her skin, showing the path of Fitzroy's tool.

"Crikey, she's sensitive," he said.

Taylor was quiet, wearing only her underpants, gazing around the room. She seemed too small to June, who was embarrassed at the dark traces of dirt that clung to the girl's shins and ankles, the Abini earth that she could never totally clean off her daughter's skin. June looked away and listened to the lab's machines humming through the walls.

When Fitzroy was done, June sat with Taylor outside on a bench and watched the sun slowly burn the clouds away. Taylor had the *Asterix* open, and she was pointing to the cartoon panels, talking quietly to herself.

"Do you want me to read them to you?" June asked. Taylor shook her head, and June began to smoke.

"I'm hungry," she said to her daughter and leaned back on the bench and let the sun cover her face. After a while she left Taylor on the bench and went inside. Fitzroy looked up at her, and he seemed confused by her presence.

"Well?" she asked.

He told her he did not know what it was, and he said that Taylor needed to see Dr. Winslow, the Australian pediatrician. June got irritated at Fitzroy's hesitation. She waited for him to voice his disapproval and say, You shouldn't have brought your child to this country. The fact that Peter didn't have a grant from his school, that she was funding his fieldwork seemed terrible right then—she wished that he had tried to get another one after he had been turned down by his department. He wouldn't even try for one of the NIH grants. She hadn't realized until now how amateurish they must seem to these British scientists. June wanted to say: Peter's project was approved—there just wasn't enough funding for it. That's not a good enough reason not to do something, is it? Not when you've got a good idea, anyway?

"But what do you *think* it is?" June asked. She brought her hands to her nose and smelled the tobacco from the Marlboro on her fingers.

"It's some kind of allergy, June. It's in her system, though. It's not really just a rash," Fitzroy said.

"Is it a worm?" she asked.

"I don't think it's a worm."

June stared at him.

"Look," he said, "this climate, this place is full of bugs and worms—ones you can see and ones you can't. The rain forest is full of bark and flowers and plants that have oils and toxins and microscopic creatures that we just don't know about yet. It is a bit like Australia in parts, but not really. That's why we're here and not in Perth or Liverpool or Pittsburgh, for that matter." He waved his hands, turning his palms up to the ceiling. "We're studying the unknown. It's exciting, but it's dangerous, you know. You must have thought about that before you left the States."

"Is it too dangerous for Taylor?" she asked.

"I don't know, June. It could be. She's so young, and she's also very sensitive."

June looked past him at the centrifuges, the steel racks of test tubes, the microscopes, the open, louvered windows.

"Is this rash—this reaction—do you think it's because we let her go off to the gardens, you know, because she runs wild around the mountains? I mean, wouldn't it be better if we kept her with us?"

"I don't know, June. I'm sorry to keep saying that, but I don't. This could be a reaction to a cat—to something she's eaten, from touching bark in the forest—it could even be a parasite from a native's skin she got from touching them."

June felt absurd then. She could see how she must seem, standing in front of him with her unbrushed hair and her too big clothes.

He looked so neat; he wore a pressed shirt and khaki pants under his lab coat. She looked down at her mud-splattered espadrilles against the linoleum floor.

"Is there anything we can do to make the hives go down?"

"Yes, cortisone cream, maybe. I'll give you some adrenaline shots. But, June, the thing about allergies—the best thing, if it's possible, is avoidance. Avoiding the allergen in the first place, I mean."

"You think we should leave?"

"That's not something I feel comfortable saying. Perhaps you should ask Dr. Winslow."

"Peter wants to stay," she said in a rush. "He doesn't want to stop his work."

"Of course," Fitzroy said. They were quiet, neither of them talking until Fitzroy drew in a breath and started: "A worry might be that she would swell internally—her throat, you see, might swell on the inside, the way the hives swell up on her skin. Or not. I'll give you the adrenaline for her, anyway."

"Would you leave?"

"I haven't got a family, June. It's just me and my research. Me and my—" he laughed, "my worms."

She saw that Tony Fitzroy was being nice. She could feel his restraint, the questions he held back. June saw him clasp his hands together, like an old woman expressing condolence. She wished that she were in Abini or Boston or even Moresby. The lab's fluorescent light and the smooth Formica tabletops made her claustrophobic.

They couldn't leave the field. It was ultimately more important for Taylor that her father stay here and complete his work, June thought. She could not imagine making him leave or the trip back to the States. What would he do then? What would it be like for the three of them back in Boston, so soon? Fitzroy wouldn't leave, either; she knew it.

They would be more careful—they would keep Taylor close to them and make sure she only ate food from the tins and boxes and jars that were shipped in from Australia and Hong Kong and Britain. They would boil the rain water, and June would make sure her daughter no longer put the steamed sweet potato and oily greens that the villagers handed her with their filth-encrusted fingers into her mouth.

June watched Fitzroy open the glass doors of a metal cabinet. He gave her tubes of cortisone, glass vials of insulin, adrenaline, and syringes. And when she said thank you, Fitzroy smiled at her and said, "Of course, of course."

...

On the way back to the guest house, June and Taylor went to Steamships. June felt relieved as she stood in the store's aisles that were full of the smell of fried meat patties coming from the lunch window that looked out onto the street. At least there was something to do now. June took a wire basket and filled it with tins of curried duck, bread pudding, and diced Indonesian ham. She closed her eyes and thought about the supply room in Abini with its shelves stacked with tinned meats and bags of rice. She needed to buy enough to protect Taylor from her allergy. When she opened her eyes, an old New Guinean man wearing a loincloth was standing next to her. He followed her as she shopped, holding a small bow and arrow, nodding as she put food in her basket.

"*Yu laik samtin?*" she asked him, slowly, angrily.

"*Nogat, misses,*" the man said, but he stayed with her, watching her put a bottle of Rose's lime cordial in the basket and then standing aside while she rifled through a bin of Chinese rubber thongs, looking for a pair small enough for Taylor. She could smell the man's skin smell and the betel nut that dyed his gums and few teeth a brilliant red. Taylor stood at her side, staring at the aisles full of canned fish, duck, and chicken. June picked up a pair of thongs and began to walk away, but her daughter stood, rooted to the spot, mesmerized by the colorful labels, the rows and rows full of dry goods.

June pushed her and snapped: "Let's go, Taylor."

The old man smiled and looked from her to Taylor. He followed them to the back of the store and then to the checkout. The cashier, a Highlands woman with a full afro, wearing the polyester blue-and-yellow Steamships uniform, began to ring up the food and thongs.

"Can't you do something about this man? He's been following me and my daughter all over your store," June said.

The cashier looked at the man and said to him in Pisin, "Go outside. You're bothering the white woman." But the old man just nodded his head and smiled.

When June and Taylor pushed the glass doors open, the man was right behind them. June handed him thirty toyah, and the coins were bright in his dark palms.

"*Apinoon, misses,*" he said and closed his fingers over the toyah.

"*Apinoon,*" June said and walked away quickly, holding the yellow plastic Steamships bag in her arms and Taylor at her side. They walked through Goroka, and June began to feel despondent as she thought about how Peter would ask her the details of what Fitzroy said. She knew that he would sit across the table from her after Taylor was asleep in her room, and he would write down the words she said on a page in the back of his notebook in his careful, beautiful handwriting. He would nod his head and agree with her, careful to say only small, quick things that would not provoke her into changing her mind and saying that they must get out of the field, that they had to leave New Guinea. She knew instead that he would sit listening so closely that the words coming from her mouth would sound strange and nonsensical to her, too, becoming so many humming breaths and stops. Nothing felt real to her.

...

Taylor got into bed and fell asleep as soon as they got back to the guest house. June put the bags from Steamships in the closet. She decided to let Taylor sleep and went downstairs. The breakfast was still laid out: tins of Milo, Nescafé, powdered milk, a pan of scrambled eggs, grilled tomatoes, and stacks of toast sat on a table near a pink plastic bucket full of Tang. June took a paper plate and spooned some eggs onto it.

She sat at an empty table in the dining room watching the anthropologists, medical workers, and newly arrived missionaries sipping their after-breakfast Nescafé. June felt the quiet disappointment in the room, the aimless, nervous glimpses at each other, at the dirty plates in front of them—what were they to do now that they were here, after months of preparation, farewell parties, vaccinations, and passport renewals? Was this it? These were the white people who could not afford the Bird of Paradise, and the shabby, clean rooms of the Lutheran guest house were a shock. The humiliating walls of class were strong and thick even here. You have not escaped the white world, she thought, and shook her head. It's stronger here.

June forced herself to stop staring. The eggs were made from powder, and they tasted chalky in her mouth. She thought about Tony Fitzroy. At that moment she wanted to stay in New Guinea, she wanted Peter to prove that he was a good scientist—that they should be in Abini—so much that her face and neck flushed red with emotion. She lit a Marlboro and ran her fingers through her hair.

And then she felt an encompassing hatred of the people in the guest house with her and decided to stay at the Bird of Paradise from now on. They were pathetic. How was it that she was with them, sitting there, while they surrounded her with their impatience and dissatisfaction? How was it that she became one of them when she was there?

Three Mayunga women wearing bright *meri* blouses with jasmine oil rubbed on their skin came into the sun-filled dining room. They seemed embarrassed to be in view of the quiet group of white people who were eating, drinking coffee, and smoking. They were holding plastic buckets and rags, and as they walked to the stairs, they filled the room with the smell of ammonia and Lux. They were speaking Pisin together and laughing, and their footsteps were loud on the stairs and then thumping through the ceiling. When the women got upstairs, they began singing a mission song,

> *Jesis luv yu na mi,*
> *yu na mi,*
> *na olgeta pikinini*

June wondered if they would wake up Taylor, if they would walk into the room and find her daughter curled up, her eyes puffy with sleep. Just then, Masta Jim, the American ex-Marine missionary who ran the guest house, walked out of the kitchen and began to sing along with the women upstairs. He stood there, sending his booming voice across the dining room. The white people looked up at him, and strained smiles covered their faces. They were awkward from his display. June wanted to shout at them, This is it—you're really here now. This is what this country is like. But she did not need to say anything. She drew deeply on her cigarette and listened to how the entire guest house was enveloped with the repetitive, plaintive song.

···

June got a tin cup from the kitchen and filled it with water and took it upstairs. She poured Rose's syrup into it and woke Taylor up. She handed her daughter the cup. The girl's skin was creased and red from the sheets. June leaned over and wiped away the sleep that had crusted to her eyelashes.

"Things are going to be different in Abini from now on," she said. "You have to stay with me and Daddy during the day."

"Why?" Taylor asked and put the cup on the nightstand.

"Taytie," she said, "you are an American girl, not a New Guinean. The bumps are allergies, they're allergies to this place, from being too close to it."

"Oh," Taylor said. "But I like to play at Tavitai and Entibe."

"I know," June said. "But you'll just have to play closer to the house. Or we'll all have to leave."

Taylor was silent.

"We're going to do school, too," she said. "We're going to do a correspondence course. Or else when you get back to Boston, all your friends will know more than you."

Taylor looked up at her mother. She seemed startled, and June thought she would say something. But then Taylor's expression changed; it was as if she left the room or turned away, but she was still in front of June. What was upsetting her, June wondered. Couldn't she remember Boston?

At that moment June was revolted by her daughter. She thought about Taylor in Abini, how she came home every day covered in dirt, her mouth full of the glottal stops and quick clicks of the native language, and the long worms coiled and curled in her large intestine that they had to flush every two months with Mebendazole. She and Peter had to hold on to her and teach her and keep her from running into the mountains.

"Taylor, you have to listen to me, or else I'm sending you to Gramma," June said.

"I don't want to go there," Taylor said.

"Okay, then you have to do the things I'm saying."

"Please let me stay here." Taylor began to cry.

June sat down on the bed next to her daughter and watched her cry. The girl's sobs got bigger until her whole body was shuddering. June held the curtain back from the window and looked at a copse of coffee trees down the road from the guest house and traced the pattern the dark green leaves made against the kunai grass.

"Come on, Taytie," she said, this time softly. "You know I'd never send you away from me." But Taylor kept crying. June lay down on the crumpled sheets where the girl had napped that morning and waited until she stopped sobbing and crawled into her arms. She fell asleep breathing in the light smell of her daughter's sweat, warmed by the strong late morning sun.

. . .

That night after dinner June took a shower in the guest house's small plastic stall. She scrubbed her ankles and her arms, until she rubbed the layer of dirt from her skin that she could never remove in the field. She combed her wet hair in the steamed bathroom mirror and saw the freckles and suntan covering her face and neck.

It was cold out, and she put on a pair of khaki pants, a long-sleeve shirt, and a pair of glass-bead earrings that she had brought with her from Boston. She held her face powder compact up to the lightbulb in the bedroom and smoothed pink lipstick onto her mouth while Taylor sat on the bed drawing on a pad with crayons. When June was done, she liked the way she looked with the brown color in her skin and her hair neat and flat.

She had decided to go out—she needed to get away from the guest house and the thoughts that had been circling in her mind since she left the British Medical Institute that morning. She craved a real drink, and she smiled at her daughter—the child would be fine for an hour. Taylor was allowed to stay up drawing for a while, her mother said, and then she must turn the lights out. June kissed her and then rubbed the lipstick off her cheek. For a moment she wanted to pull the girl into her and feel her skin and her heart beating in her chest. But instead she pulled Taylor's pajama top up and looked at the rash; the bumps seemed smaller. We three are over-wrought, she decided; everything is fine.

June walked through the Lutheran guest house's garden into the night. She thought about Peter then, sketching in his journal, listening to the BBC on his shortwave radio, sipping milky Lapsang Souchong. He should have insisted on coming with her. She was completely tired then; she felt like she had run a marathon or swum around an island. She reached up and felt her neatly combed wet hair and lit a cigarette.

She walked past the houses of New Guineans that she barely noticed during the day. They were flimsy structures, propped up on stilts Milne Bay style, and at night their cooking fires illumi-nated the aluminum-siding walls and sent an orange glow and the peculiar smell of wood smoke mingled with steaming rice and jack mackerel into the darkness. She breathed in the air and felt how she was a little dizzy from the nicotine and the mountain air.

June smiled when she saw the flaming torches that lit up the Bird of Paradise's entry. She wondered if they thought their guests would be reminded of a trip to Tahiti or a resort in Madang. She walked around the side of the hotel, feeling the rough stucco under her fingertips. The stairs that led down to the bar were painted aqua surrounded by pink bougainvillea. She wanted a drink, and she decided that she liked how the Bird pretended it was somewhere else, fun and light and easy.

When she got down the stairs, she saw Tony Fitzroy sitting at a round table with Jordy King, a researcher from the British Insti-tute. She waved at them and smiled and felt them take in her pres-ence: her lipstick, wet hair, and smile.

She got a drink and sat at Fitzroy's table, adjusting to the flat fluorescence after the pure color of the moonless night lit by the

Bird of Paradise's torches. She wondered if Fitzroy had told everyone at the Institute about her visit with Taylor, and she watched Jordy King while he talked to Fitzroy. The two men discussed a paper Fitzroy had read in Brisbane. June listened to them, feeling the acid taste of tinned pineapple juice and vodka in her mouth. She got up and ordered another one and imagined walking into the Lutheran guest house late, smelling of vodka. As the drink settled in her stomach, she was embarrassed that they were ignoring her so casually. Poor Taylor, she thought, and was surprised at herself. The image of her daughter was strong right then.

"How's it going for you two in Abini?" Jordy asked when she got back to the table. He was hunched over his beer, smiling up at her.

"Hasn't Tony told you? We're three," June said.

"That's right, you've got a child with you," Jordy said and nodded at his beer.

He was wearing a white turtleneck under a khaki shirt. Safari wear, June thought. When she had met Jordy at the British Institute, she noticed him only enough to see that he was competitive with Peter in front of Fitzroy. He irritated her, and she had wanted to be alone with Fitzroy. She felt compelled to explain something to him, to impress her presence on him. She looked around the bar, trying to communicate her displeasure to Jordy King.

"We've got our daughter, Taylor, with us," she said.

"You three enjoying it, then?"

June looked over at Fitzroy. "It's evah so lovely," she said, affecting a British accent. She felt excited by her dislike of Jordy King and bold from the vodka. "There are simply scads of the most fabulous diseases."

Jordy and Fitzroy laughed.

"You're tired, June. I can see it in your face," Fitzroy said.

"Is that right?" June asked. "I sort of thought I was looking well."

As soon as she spoke, she knew it was the wrong thing to say. She saw the bar with its snooker table and these two men, drinking, wanting to be alone, disapproving of her, as though she were far away. And she saw herself, too, and could only watch in dismay as she sputtered the wrong thing.

She knew then that Fitzroy hadn't told Jordy anything about her or Taylor. She saw how uncomfortable she was making him. She saw her mistake: his standing invitation to drink at the Bird, issued when they first got to Goroka, had been to her and Peter, not her alone. Of course, she thought, he thinks I'm upset. June looked over at the snooker tables and the bamboo bar. She was the only woman in the room. She closed her eyes and felt the alcohol and wished she had eaten more with Taylor at the guest house dinner.

"No, you're right," she said. She swallowed the rest of her drink and saw how the sediment from the pineapple juice stuck to the glass. "I seem to be too tired since I left the field. I slept all afternoon."

"It's not so bad. We all get a bit tropo out here," Jordy said.

He looked ridiculous to her in the fluorescence, and she was peeved that he was trying to be reassuring. The three of them were silent for a while, and June lit a cigarette and began smoking.

"It's funny for me to be at the Lutheran guest house," June said. She felt nervous and thought about having another vodka, but she knew that would make her drunk. It was so important right then that Fitzroy would like her.

"Why's that?" he asked.

"Well, you know, since I'm Jewish. I keep waiting for Masta Jim to say something." She saw Fitzroy raise his eyebrows. She knew they had thought it about her. "Even Peter's last name isn't much of a disguise when you're dealing with the likes of the Lutherans. What gives me away, though? I keep trying to figure it out. Is it my dark hair?" she laughed. "Or my tendency to avoid the bacon at breakfast?"

The two men looked startled, but then filled their expressions with polite smiles.

"If you're uncomfortable, June, you three can stay at the Institute. We have space for visiting scientists. You know, little apartments with baths and kitchens," Fitzroy said.

June listened to his words: you three. There it was, Peter was always the ticket inside with the world at large and with her, too. Where was he?

"Oh, I wasn't looking for an invitation," she said. "But that's nice."

"Of course," Fitzroy said and took a sip of his beer. Jordy smiled at her.

"How's your daughter finding life in the bush?" Jordy asked. "I know some S.I.L. folks whose kids had a hard time."

"Did they?" June asked.

"Sure, it's tough—the culture gap, the language, the sun. Kids get lonely in the bush. To say nothing of the parents, ha ha." Jordy laughed and brought his beer to his mouth. He winked at June farcically as he put the glass on the table.

"My daughter seems not to be having a difficult enough time," June laughed. "She's catching all the native bugs and worms, right, Tony?"

"I don't know, June," Fitzroy said.

"You must think I'm a terrible mother." She felt high from the vodka, and again she wished that Jordy would leave.

"I think that you and Peter are giving Taylor a wonderful opportunity," Fitzroy said.

"God, you Englishmen never let on what you really think," June said. She felt like bursting into tears. She raised her glass and shouted, "Hail, Britannia!"

"Good lord, June," Fitzroy said. "Really."

"You forget," Jordy said, laughing, "one doesn't want to salute the Union Jack all that vocally around here. We're surrounded by hostile Aussies."

June stared at Fitzroy and then said quietly: "I'm sorry. I think it is tough for me."

"It's tough for all of us," Fitzroy said.

His expression was so kind that June thought she would cry. It seemed as though he knew everything and was able to classify and diminish the power of the place over her husband and her daughter and herself. June reached across the table and placed the tips of her fingers on his. Fitzroy pulled his hand back from hers and said, "Oh."

June was sitting there then with her hand palm down on the wood table in front of him. She was completely embarrassed. She was nothing in Fitzroy's world; she had no slot, no category. She was just a white woman with a sick child. Maybe he did not even think she was that white anymore now that she had declared her Jewishness. Paranoid, is what Peter would say. You're being paranoid.

"I'm going back," she said, directing her gaze at Fitzroy. "I've got to get back to Taytie."

Jordy raised his beer to her and said, "Good night then, June."

June stood up and looked at the two men. She wanted to stay with them. She hated Goroka and the guest house. She felt an enormous wave of homesickness fill her body. It had taken only two drinks for the loneliness to crawl up, leaving her exposed. She should not have drunk anything without Peter there to help her navigate the place.

She thought about sitting down and having another drink, but both men had made their relief too clear when she said she was leaving.

"Good night, fellows," June said, and as soon as the words were out of her mouth she was bothered by how wistful she sounded.

...

When June got to the guest house, she pushed open the gate and sat down in the garden. She leaned back on her hands and looked up at the windows on the second floor and counted over to the room where Taylor was sleeping. She wanted to call to the girl, to shout until her daughter woke up and flicked on the fluorescent light and put her face to the window.

The wet garden soil dampened her pants. She thought about Fitzroy and Jordy King sitting at the bar. What were they saying about her right now? She dug her fingers under a flowering impatiens and felt the delicate, slight roots that it clung to the soil with, like a subterranean spiderweb. She looked up at the house and saw a man standing on the porch.

"Good evening, Mrs. Campbell," he said. It was Masta Jim, standing in his bathrobe and a pair of flip-flops.

"Hello, Jim," June said. The expatriates in Goroka called the missionary Jim to his face, Masta Jim behind his back and to New Guineans. "I've just been over at the Bird."

Masta Jim nodded and walked off the porch. He pointed up at the house to the foil-encrusted panels that sat on the roof.

"They're solar panels," he said to her in his slow, southern drawl. "I heat the water for the guest house and the school with them."

"Yes," June said. "I've seen them before. Very efficient." She wanted to laugh. Masta Jim was a caricature to her. She thought about telling Peter this story, describing the scene: the darkness, the missionary in his bathrobe, catching her with her hands en-

trenched in his flower patch. He was nodding up at the roof, smiling at the solar panels.

June reached behind her and began to ease her weight onto
her feet. As she stood up, Masta Jim cleared his throat.

"Mrs. Campbell, may I ask you a personal question?"

"Of course, Jim," she said. She was dizzy from standing up,
and she felt cold and thick with the alcohol on her tongue and in
her blood. She brushed her dirt-covered hands on her pants.

"Why did you leave your daughter alone tonight?"

June stared at Masta Jim through the dark. She thought of the
Abini mission she and Peter had gone to when they first arrived in
the field: *Debil em papa pope na ol lain Hebreu.* The devil is the pope
and the Hebrews. The phrase was loud in her mind. She thought
of Taylor in her bed asleep in sheets that were boiled and bleached
by Masta Jim's Mayunga women. Goroka was cold at night, high
up in the mountains like Abini, and June wrapped her arms around
her chest, covering her breasts.

"I don't think that's a fair question to ask. It's not your
business."

"I know," Masta Jim said. "But I asked it."

"Do you have a problem with me staying here?" June asked.

She felt light-headed. She looked up at the guest house—she
would wake up Taylor and call Tony Fitzroy. But even as she felt
the panic begin to circle in her mind, she knew there was no dan-
ger. Nothing was wrong, he was just nosey or bored. It was flat,
even, as unfulfilling as the conversation with Fitzroy and Jordy King.

"No, nothing like that," he said. "I was just wondering, is all."

"I don't have to answer your questions," she said. "You're
prying."

"Mrs. Campbell, I'm a missionary. I care for you and your
daughter and all of God's children."

June stood and stared at Masta Jim. She could see his features, his short blond hair through the dark. Would he do this if Peter were there? If she were not a Jew?

"Love never ends," he said, breaking the quiet with his slow drawl. "As for prophecies, they will pass away; as for tongues, they will cease; as for knowledge, it will pass away."

"I can't believe you," June said. "I really cannot believe you. Do you think I'm some *kanaka,* scared of you?"

"Look, Mrs. Campbell, I didn't mean to upset you so much."

"You haven't," she said.

"Good," he said. "I heard your daughter tonight, sniffling and snuffling, in her room. That's all."

"Oh, God," June said, her heart sinking.

"Gut nait," Masta Jim said and stayed out on the porch while she went inside.

...

When June walked inside the guest house, its smell of disinfectant and old books seemed impossibly light to her. Without meaning to, she drew in deep breaths, capturing the building's essence with her nose and lungs. She got into bed with Taylor and held her daughter against her chest, between her legs, waking the girl up and then kissing her cheek, her mouth, her nose. The child blinked and gazed up at her mother from her dream and then rubbed her eyes and went back to sleep.

June stayed awake in the guest house's cold bedroom, thinking about the night at the Bird of Paradise and then the conversation with Masta Jim. Taylor looked so much like Peter, it always surprised and then pleased her. She ran her fingers along her daughter's face, tracing her features. Taylor did not alarm her; that night in Goroka her daughter was as clear to her as her own body. As dawn broke she thought about sending Taylor back to Boston to live with her mother. But she knew she would not.

...

In the morning June got dressed and put a bandanna over her hair. She walked to the ANZ bank and withdrew two hundred kina from her account. She tucked the envelope full of cash into her skirt and went to the airstrip and hired a helicopter to fly her and Taylor to Abini. On her way back to the guest house, June imagined how she would pack for her daughter's allergy: she pictured the aluminum tubes of antihistamine, cortisone, and pink Calamine lotion she bought from the Chessing Pharmacy, the delicate vials of adrenaline and insulin and plastic-wrapped syringes that Fitzroy gave her. She nodded unconsciously and thought how they would keep Taylor close to the compound during the day and bathe her with Phisoderm in the afternoon, before the rains when green-filtered light poured through the fiberglass roof panel over the shower stall and June would be able to see her daughter's skin clearly.

And later that morning as the helicopter lifted June, her daughter, and a box of dry goods from Steamships up over Goroka, she watched the neat pattern of buildings the Australians had planned from the air. The district officer's residence sat wide and enormous at the spine of a fan that spread out to the post office, the court building, the medical center, and the airstrip. She saw the yellow and blue square of Steamships, the dark red buildings of the British Medical Institute, the turquoise Goroka pool, and finally the polo club, its lawns cut out from the kunai-covered foothills at the southern end of the town.

The dense green of the rain forest spread beneath them, and the mountains became larger and clustered together as they went farther east. They flew over hamlets that were cut out of mountain ridges, their circular thatch roofs and orange earth floors distinct against the endless forest. June turned around and looked at Taylor, crouched in the back of the Sikorsky, the gray earphones dwarfing her head. She was gazing out the window, down at the amphitheaters of mountains and the rocks that jutted out and the waterfalls that fell hundreds of feet into oblivion.

Taylor was mouthing words to herself, inaudible over the enormous noise of the helicopter. June wondered if she were speaking English or Abini. She wanted to crawl into the back seat and hold the girl. Taylor was odd to her then, and even ugly, with her sunburned skin, her unevenly cut hair, and the smell of the cortisone and the guest house's soap surrounding her. Taylor was like a photograph of a young Peter, with her fair hair that curled around her wide face. June had never seen anything of herself in her daughter. She used to joke with her mother that Taylor was like a visiting dignitary when she was a toddler, quiet and neat and polite.

The helicopter hovered over the landing circle in Abini. A crowd of villagers had gathered, and they crouched together, waving up at the Sikorsky's plastic bubble while they were blown by the rotor's intense wind into the bamboo stands planted near the landing. June felt adrenaline pump through her blood when she saw her husband. She waved at Peter, who looked impossibly tall among the villagers. When they landed, June opened the helicopter door, turned around, and took her daughter's hand. She smiled at the crowd that had gathered to meet them and bent over Taylor and kissed her scalp, breathing in the girl's body smell. The morning clouds had not yet burned off of Mt. Abini. They hung thick and blue around the peak, and the mountain's tree cover was blurred. But she knew the view would be clear by noon.

S E V E N

When he thought about it later, Peter could not decide whether
Makino Butu had brought him to the regrowth forest at the bottom of Mt. Philip deliberately. Makino lived close to the Campbells'
compound, in Beriapi, and had been friendly but had rarely spoken to Peter, so when he had come by the compound, unexpect-
edly, and talked about bower birds that built elaborate stages out of
twigs and moss and decorated them with orchids and wild ginger
flowers, Peter had been excited and eager to go with him. The New
Guinean said that the bird hopped, danced, and sang as he waited
for a mate and told Peter to bring his camera. Makino had stood on
the lawn in the flat morning light and pantomimed pressing the
shutter and then winding the film. Everything I do is watched, Peter
thought.

The two of them had left before dawn and spent the morning sitting on a tari root, watching the immaculately groomed bower. The bird never came, and Peter sat quietly with the Nikon on his lap, occasionally taking photos of the bower and then of Makino sitting on the moss-covered forest floor looking grimly at the bird's empty stage.

Just before noon, when they agreed to go home, Makino rolled a cigarette out of newsprint and braided dry-store tobacco, and the two men shared it, passing it back and forth until it was wet with spit. They walked back toward the compound, around the side of the mountain through an overgrown garden. The path twisted out of the garden and followed the Abini river through a grove of cardamom trees. Peter crouched down and took a photo of the river flowing over its rock bed.

"Wait," Makino hissed. "Listen." He stopped short on the path, and Peter almost collided with him.

They stood there in the sun, and Peter could hear only the sound of the Abini crashing and a woman calling out in the far distance.

"A bird?" Peter asked, whispering.

"*Nogat,*" Makino shook his head furiously. And then: "Do you hear?"

And then, gradually, Peter heard—the sound of footsteps on leaves, whispers, a cough. He felt goose bumps on his arms and thighs, and he shook his head. Something was wrong.

Then, in the next moment, Makino began shouting in Abini. Two boys, one with a light beard covering his face, the other wearing only a pair of ratty shorts, darted out from a stand of bamboo trees. Peter was confused. It was as if the boys had appeared out of thin air. The images in front of him were swirling, a rush of green and brown that moved so fast that Peter could not make sense out of what was happening. Makino reached out and grabbed the younger boy by the ear and smacked him in the face, all the while shouting, filling the tree canopy with his voice. The older boy, the bearded one, looked at Peter and then ran away, his feet barely touching the roots and rocks beneath him.

"*Lukim, masta,*" Makino said, breathing hard.

Peter saw his daughter hiding in the dense brush of the cardamom grove. He felt like he had walked into a dream. The blue bandanna that June tied around her hair every morning was lying on the ground in front of him. He felt sick. Is this why she was full of rashes and allergies and worms and splinters under her delicate pink skin? It was natural, he thought, for her to want to play and touch but how could he explain to her that she couldn't do that here?

"Taylor?" he asked. "What are you doing?"

The boy standing with Makino began to cry a low, whining sob. Peter knew that the children were terrified of him—his height, his whiteness, his blue eyes—his presence was too much to be up close to. He knew also that Taylor occasionally used the threat of calling him to bully her friends into doing what she wanted.

"Tay," he said, upset, "You know Mommy said you weren't to go so far from home anymore."

The girl was silent, refusing to look at him. Somewhere in his mind Peter knew that Makino was standing behind him, watching. What was it that he was supposed to see? Did Makino want him to get angry at his daughter?

"Taylor," Peter said. "Come here."

He was shocked that she was not afraid of him. It occurred to him that he and June did not really know her anymore—she was full of secrets, hiding in the thousands of crevices and clearings and abandoned gardens of the Abini rain forest.

"What are you doing up here?" he asked, but he did not mean for her to answer and she didn't. He forced his mind to see what was in front of him: the moss-covered ground, the blue sky high above the tree line, the ginger plants that had been bruised and knocked over by their quick strides, the cardamom grove overgrown with vines and saplings, his daughter trying to melt into this impossible landscape, and the body heat from Makino behind him and the boy he held, who was whimpering, caught by his wrists.

Peter felt that this had happened already, that this was repetition that he could not understand. He thought that he had caused this, that he sent his daughter out here into this world that she could only stumble through blindly. He looked at her face and arms that were covered with streaks of sap and dirt. This was how she looked when she came home before June put her in the bath.

"You mustn't do this," he said. "It's wrong."

"I'm not doing anything, Daddy," she said, defiantly.

He walked across the clearing then and grabbed her arm. Touching her skin, he was alarmed by how sturdy she was. This place, the earth, the incessant rains, the rain forest that encompassed every being within it, had permeated her, changed her, until now she was so different from him.

"Taylor, you must not come up into the forest alone with boys. You must not."

He ran his fingers through his hair, feeling the sweat from his scalp. He thought: We should never have brought her here. How could he explain rules to his daughter in this world? It wasn't just for her, either—he could sense how upset Makino was. Just then the boy shouted and pulled away from Makino's grasp and ran down the path. They watched his legs pumping, running as he disappeared.

"*Ai,*" Makino said. "*Sori.*"

"You have to understand, Taylor, that these people don't realize what you're doing. They don't know what you mean. You're different than they are," Peter said softly. But as soon as his words were out in the day, he knew they were confusing, and he wasn't sure what he meant. I'm overreacting, he thought. They were just playing. And it is different here.

Peter picked up Taylor and carried her down the path. The light through the trees threw delicate patterns on the ground. The three of them walked in silence. As they got closer to the compound, they heard sounds from Beriapi, a baby crying, a pig snorting, a woman yelling at her child, floating across the forever of the Abini valley.

Taylor was resting her head on her father's shoulder, and she began humming a tuneless song, singing Abini words: *"Biri mine nao kao ke way ke way."* Peter asked in Pisin what she was singing. Taylor was silent and rubbed her palm to her eyes.

"A children's song," Makino said in Pisin. "Nonsense words."

When they got to the compound, Peter put his daughter down. His back hurt, and he stretched his arms up. He watched Taylor walk up the wide steps. June opened the door, looked out at him and then down at the girl. Without saying anything she wrapped her arms around her daughter and met Peter's gaze, her eyes full of confusion and worry.

"What?" she mouthed.

Peter shook his head. He could tell, even from a distance, that Taylor was stiff in her mother's arms, not weeping, not scared.

Abini Village
April 16

Dear Professor Morris,

I hope this letter finds you in good health and everything going smoothly at the university. June and I are nearing completion of the first background survey. It has proved a more difficult task than I projected in my last letter for a variety of reasons. Among the many logistical stumbling blocks is our inability to navigate the native language. Although most men here speak Pisin, almost none of the women do, so we find ourselves hiring assorted men to interpret when we survey the women and children. We usually get incorrect information or at least have huge gaps in the data, e.g. (me, looking at my notes): "I thought you said this woman had two children." (Interpreter, frustrated): "No, two sons. She has five children altogether." This results in our daily work consisting of a most painstaking process of revision, checking, and double checking for basic census/kinship stuff, which I think is vital to see patterns of genetic disease, among other things. Also, in the Abini cosmos people don't die from illness, they are only ever murdered by "poison." Whenever I ask how someone died, their symptoms, etc., the answer is always a variation on: "Oh, he died of very strong poison, his enemy from Malvi got a piece of his hair when he was at a wedding feast and not paying attention."

I have enclosed some photos of the most common ailments we're encountering, which are mostly dermatological. In fact, aside from what I suspect is a case of leukemia, we have found very little (obvious) serious illness. This is not to say that your average Abini resident isn't a walking host of an extraordinary number of parasites, tropical ulcers, rashes, candidiasis, severe tooth decay, chronic dysentery, and head, body, and pubic lice. Most of the juvenile population exhibits classic symptoms of malnutrition (see the photos I've labeled 4a and 4b). From what we've witnessed and heard anecdotally, there is also a high infant mortality rate. All of which we expected.

We hope to begin collecting blood samples by early next month, when the generator is supposed to arrive. We had a small refrigerator flown in, but getting hold of the generator has proven a nightmarish exercise. Tony Fitzroy at the BMI continues to be most helpful and kind; he speaks highly of you and sends his best wishes, as do I.

Yours truly,
Peter Campbell

Peter told June that Makino had taken him to a cardamom grove at the edge of an abandoned, overgrown garden. He told her about his confusion and the scuffle in the thick, green trees and then the two boys, running into the daylight, tussling with Makino, and then Taylor's emergence, her strange, angry demeanor, her refusal to talk to him. June began to cry, and she vomited into the kitchen sink. Peter was silent while she rinsed her face and dried it with a tea towel and then lit a Marlboro.

"I can't stand this," she said to him. "I can't."

Peter looked at her face, the details of her body: the wide hips, her incessant smoking, sucking on the filter tip of her cigarette. She irritated him then. Her mannerisms had become extreme in the field—her nagging, the paranoia about germs and the villagers—it was all self-parody, and Peter hated it. He still wanted to talk to her, to find her and discuss Taylor, the boys, what Makino must have told everyone, but she would not do it. He stood watching her smoke.

"Well," she said, "this is impossible. We have to leave."

"It isn't," he said. "I don't think we have to. We don't even know what really happened."

"I can't even talk to you. You're not even here, Peter."

"I am, June," he said. "I see it. It's almost—in a way, it's almost natural. Kids play, come on, you know that, everyone does." Peter shrugged.

"She won't even listen to us. She won't even stay close to the house like she's supposed to, like Tony Fitzroy—she's going to keep getting that rash, Peter."

"Taylor's okay, really she is. Look where we are. How can we ask her not to really be here? To stay in the compound all day like some missionary's kid?"

"You just don't want to leave, do you?"

"June, I really don't think we need to do that yet."

"It's on you then."

"I know it is," he said. "That's fine."

Abini

May 2

Dear Mother and Dad,

Thanks so much for your wonderful "care package." Taylor loves the doll (she has named her Juliette), and the clothes were a terrific thought, as her wardrobe was getting a bit ratty. Her allergic reaction—the bumps, as she calls them—has gone down and not returned, so for now we are crossing our fingers that it was a once only deal.

As for our work, it is going okay, but June and I are often frustrated at the end of the day. It is exhausting to hike to remote hamlets weighed down by equipment in the unrelenting heat and glare of this sun. And very often I feel like I am getting so little done of even the most basic nature. Enough complaining; this place is magnificent, and our vegetable garden is sprouting the most incredible harvest. A patrol officer in Goroka told me that all you have to do is plant your seeds and get out of the way, and he is right! Our cucumbers, tomatoes, cabbages, and eggplants are huge and delicious. In addition, our chicken coop (*haus kakaruk* in Pisin) is in fine form. We started out with two hens and a rooster and now have something like eighteen chickens of various ages. Tay has named them all, of course, so they really function as pets rather than protein. Oh, well.

Tay herself has been given an Abini name (Mori—it means little flower), and up until now she has spent most of her days away from us. It is remarkable how much she has adapted to the place; she almost seems more of Abini than Boston. She speaks the language fluently and comes home in the evening dressed up in orchids and poinsettia singing these funny little ditties.

"What's that song?" I asked her yesterday. She looked at me with pity and then said enigmatically, "It's about a rock in a river, Daddy." June and I worry that her transition back to civilization might be tough. We've been here so long that her reading and writing skills are slipping from her—but June has ordered away for an Australian correspondence course, and we're going to try and teach her ourselves—and her command of spoken English isn't as firm as we'd like. But children adapt, and anyway there are moments when she is helping me in the garden or playing with Juliette when she turns and smiles and looks just like an ordinary American girl, and I know all will be okay in the end.

In addition to the beloved Juliette, Taylor has a piglet! It is actually quite adorable. She's named it Edgar Oranges, and it follows her around squeaking and grunting when we pet its little pink belly. June and I have said that it's okay for Edgar to sleep in Taylor's room for a while, and we now have little gruntings and snorts to lull us to sleep. How weird this life I'm living must seem to you. It's bizarre for me, too, sometimes. It feels like a dream, especially at sunset after the rains when the sky swells and the most intense hues of purple, orange, and red blanket the mountains and valleys. Love to you from June and Taylor and of course, all of my love,

Peter

Peter and June decided together that June would stay in the compound during the day for a few weeks and teach Taylor to read from the Queensland Correspondence School's thin books, with their red covers and wide, large, blue-printed letters. And during those days, in the gray mornings when the steam of night clouds still clung to the compound's ground, Taylor's friends Pende and Tilani would arrive. They sat by the back door talking in quiet voices, giggling and hugging their chests when Peter or June emerged to go to the outhouse. They waited there, like that, while the Campbells had their breakfast and June washed the dishes. Then the two of them crawled under the house and sat right below the kitchen table playing jacks with river pebbles, whispering and laughing, while Taylor sat above them with her mother, learning how to read.

Taylor was frustrated by the work of memorizing letters and words and reading through the correspondence school's nonsensical rhyming stories. Eventually, she refused to do any work. She would sit in her room then, alone with picture books, listening to her friends below the house making the soft sounds of Abini and clicking their game pebbles together.

And later in the day June told Peter that it wasn't until lunch time that she allowed the two girls to come inside and sit, squatting on the bamboo floor, eating biscuits covered with Tiptree strawberry preserves while Taylor ate a tuna-fish sandwich or bread and peanut butter. The girls would leave the compound promising to stay close, promising to be back before the afternoon rains started. June would do the wash then, squeezing Lux and boiling water into the woven cotton of their clothes, rinsing and wringing them into the little stream that ran across the compound, and then hanging them on the line, while she watched for the rain clouds, waiting for Taylor and Peter to come home.

May 29
Abini

Dear Tom,

It was great to get your letter and the pics of you and Susan in the Rockies. What a trip that must have been! Things are moving right along here in the bush, although maybe that isn't exactly true, as time has a completely different feel here than it

does in the good ole US of A. The Abini have one word that
means today and one word that means yesterday, tomorrow, and
all future time. According to Tay, my resident Abini linguist, it's
not confusing at all to the Abini—you just indicate the event
you're talking about, and the word's role as either yesterday or
tomorrow becomes clear. Hmmm, I don't get it myself, but I do
know that the rain forest and the mountains and the daily
downpours make you feel as though time is an entity like space,
just as Al Einstein said it was.

In answer to your question about me and June being
isolated—yes and no. In a weird way we're more distant than
ever—Taylor's allergies and worms and assorted other episodes
have been really hard on us—but I'm also discovering this
intense and primitive bond between us, as though we're a
brother-and-sister couple, like Pharaoh and his queen, who were
always brother and sister and man and wife. (Uh oh—delusions
of grandeur have set in!) We don't have sex anymore, really, as
we have no sound privacy (all the walls are bamboo), and we
sleep in separate, narrow cots. We seem to have become closer
and farther apart here in Abini, and sometimes I do wonder if
we are the right people for each other. But I can't imagine life
without June at my side. She is fragile, which I knew when I
married her. Sometimes I feel more protective and concerned for
her than I do for Taylor, who is essentially a hardy soul.

She and Taylor fight a lot now, especially as she is trying to
teach Taylor to read, which is quickly seeming an impossible,
frustrating task. I am the referee; after a big fight it is my job to
go hunt for Taylor, who hides with her pig, Edgar, and I invari-
ably come upon the two of them stewing, furious at June, in a
far reach of our compound. Edgar, the catalyst for many a
mother-daughter skirmish, now has a leash and sleeps in the
front of the house as a compromise. However, between you and

me, I have caught Taylor snoring away next to him a few nights in a row.

We had a lot of excitement recently when a patrol officer visited. Patrol officers are young, godlike, brawny Australian men who trek through the rain-forested Highlands outfitted in *haute* colonial gear with fifty carriers humping metal "government boxes" in their wake. They're called *kiaps* in Pisin, and it's quite an event when they roll into a remote village like Abini. The *kiap* who visited us, Craig Michaels, whipped out a folding chair, put on his bush hat, and dispensed justice for a few hours before dinner. It amazes me that the people here abide by his decisions, but they do. One fellow had to give his neighbor two ax heads and a chicken to pay for damage one of his pigs did to a garden fence. Craig also dealt with a scandal that's been rocking Abini for weeks. He decreed the punishment for an adulterous couple—the sinning man and woman were ordered never to be alone together, and the woman's infant boy, widely believed to be her lover's, not her husband's, was taken away from her. We'll see how that one works.

After dinner, Craig talked about seeing Carleton Gajdusek in Kainantu, operating his medical research with the full financial backing of the U.S. government, which has made quite an impression on the locals (Australian and PNGers). Gajdusek had tons of medical equipment and helicopters and trucks and various foreign scientists swooping in. It was interesting to listen to Craig tell the kuru story, though I already knew it. I knew it from medical journals and lectures, not from the *kiap*'s perspective. Tay and June were rapt as he talked about how people with kuru become palsied and demented, and how almost all of the victims of the gruesome viral disease are women and children because they are the cannibals and eat the infectious, diseased brains. Nothing that exciting is going on in Abini, I'm afraid.

I'm supposed to go into the rain forest with a few village men in a week or two to see birds of paradise and what they call the "true bush." Anyway, buddy, keep the letters flowing. It's great to have news of home—it makes me feel closer to the real world.

Lots of love,
Peter

Mt. Philip rain forest
June 10

Dear Mother and Dad,

I wish that you could see where I am. I will try to explain it to you, but words are so lame, aren't they? I am sitting in a clearing in the rain forest under a shelter made from leafy, wild ginger plants. The men I'm with cut down a circle of trees this morning and let the sun into the dark, wet greenness. The sunlight flattens the forest—usually the diffuse green glow makes the moss-carpeted floor and the rocks and vines seem full of a hundred thousand hollows and crevices. But now I can see mushrooms that cling to green bark, spreading their translucent bodies across the tree, and brilliant red orchids that sneak up hanging vines. When the men chopped open one of the trees, it was full of enormous white maggots that were burrowing blindly through the soft, rotting flesh of the trunk. Tay (I brought her with me) was delighted and crouched over the chopped apart tree with two of her friends and scooped the creatures out and then roasted them over a small fire until they had a crisp, black skin and then popped them in their mouths. She says they are delicious, but I have yet to try one.

It took us a solid day of hiking to get up here. When we first left Abini, we walked mostly through light regrowth forest, which is land that was originally cleared for a garden and allowed to go wild when the soil was no longer fertile. But eventually we came to the "true bush," which is dense and filled with this exquisite wet smell and orchids and vines that hang from a cathedral of forty- and fifty-foot trees. Really, I felt religious for the first time in my life. Ah ha, thought I, this is how a medieval peasant felt when he first walked into an ornate Catholic church, full of stained-glass windows and jewel-encrusted relics. I believe! And when the rains came, we were all soaked, although Tay and I were the only two in shoes and clothes, so of course we stayed wet much longer than anyone else. It is amazing to watch our guides navigate barefoot over slick logs, moss-covered rocks, thick roots and vines. Their bare feet with splayed, broken toes slap the ground with such assurance. They never seem to slip or slow down, not even the children, while Taylor and I spent most of the walk grasping tree branches and steadying ourselves with our arms stuck out like amateur tightrope walkers.

As we walked deeper and deeper into the forest, the most incredible symphony of bird calls, waterfalls, insect buzzing, and wind whistling through the trees surrounded us. The sound is all encompassing, and it is hard for me to believe that this music is not deliberate. I must say that now I am in an amazed, trancelike state at nature, Darwin seems obscene. How could he have come up with such an unromantic and dyspeptic theory in a place as lovely as the Galapagos? I would understand better if he had been in Liverpool or Birmingham. Yet, the sad thing is that I am a scientist, and I do believe that all of this really is about coincidence and survival of the fittest. Or, so I say to you.

I am watching Tay right now talking to her friends. They have found a treasure trove of startled insects and spiders who no longer have tree cover to hide behind. A wave of yellow butterflies is swirling above them, and they are gathering quite scary-looking (to me) iridescent beetles in their hands.

I don't know—thought seems to me the only pure thing in the world. It's only when we act, and we do, we always do, that things get ugly and corrupt. But how absurd you must think I'm being, but can you sort of see what I mean? Contemplation is fine—it's only when one goes out and imposes ideas of how things should be, that the trouble starts. Better to approach the world observing and passive.

Here in the Eastern Highlands existence is more awesome and difficult than anything I ever conceived of in the States. What can I do? I look at Taylor, who is only seven, and she is already complex, difficult, full of secrets, and much more interested in this place than in either me or June. Part of me agrees with her wholeheartedly, silently encouraging her to shed herself, her thoughts, her Americanness, and just become something different than herself. But what I know is that she never can; I know she never will.

I'm going to end on that note, not that I don't have a million more things I would like to tell you, but I am tired from the hike, and we are to head back this afternoon. I need to take a nap. I love you,

Petey

29 JUNE
TO: MR. AND MRS. T. CAMPBELL
BOSTON, MA/USA
FROM: CAMPBELL /c/o/ BMI/ GOROKA, EHP, PAPUA
NEW GUINEA
TELEX NO: 06321754

We 3 are taking R&R in Madang STOP generator broke blood samples ruined STOP all
healthy letter soon STOP
P, J, & T

July 17
Abini Village

Dear Tom,

We've been in Madang—a beach resort on the coast that looks a bit like Hawaii—for two weeks, getting some badly needed relaxation. It was such a treat to get to Goroka and find your letters and all the copies of *Time* you sent. All three of us have spent hours with them. The news, photos, and ads (especially the ads) are so exotic to us, like tidings from a civilization on another planet.

You heard right—all the blood samples spoiled when the generator gave out. I feel like throwing up, and I have since I opened our little refrigerator and felt warmth emanating from it. We have to start again, I suppose, but I'm thinking about writing to my advisor and hinting that maybe a blood survey won't be part of my data. I realize how shoddy that would make my work seem, though, and thinking about it makes me so frustrated. Essentially then, I will have completed a glorified census, reduplicating information the Australian government has already gathered.

I've been wondering why we did come here. I thought about it a lot when we were in Madang, when I watched Tay splashing in the pool, drinking Coca-Cola, and coloring in her coloring books. As soon as we were out of the field, everything calmed down between the three of us. Getting out of Abini made me see how intense and exaggerated our existence is here. I have worked under the assumption that this life in New

Guinea isn't exactly real; real life is Cambridge, graduate school, my parents' house, etc. But now I wonder if this isn't also real, and if the intensity, the freakishness of the place isn't exactly why June and I came here. In many ways, I think we decided to come here so far away from home, from the familiar, to get closer to each other, to penetrate the thick membrane that separated us from each other in "civilization." But when I look closely at her, I see good and bad things, but I do not feel desire for her to be in my skin. I don't think either of us really wants to dissolve that membrane. I worry that Taylor suffers for us, that she has the passion of a child born to parents who can't really love each other. (I suppose this is what they call going "tropo"—a.k.a. the white man's freak-out.)

Since we've been back in the field, the fights between Tay and June have gotten more and more horrendous. June and I thought that this kind of warring wouldn't start until Tay was an adolescent. She has basically completely refused to continue learning to read or write English. We have given up this particular fight with her—she will be able to pick it up with a tutor when we get back to the USA, don't you agree?

I think that perhaps the soil here, which makes our American seeds grow so quickly into lush vegetables, has had a similar effect on my daughter. She acts like a teenager—moody, quiet, and sulky. For some reason ("some reason?" I hear June shout) I am Switzerland, and Tay will sit with me behaving well, quite adorably even, helping or asking questions.

Right when we got back from Madang there was a terrible incident with Edgar Oranges Campbell, Tay's pig. The woman, Nari, who gave Edgar to Tay, came to say that she needed him back. He'd grown big and fat, and, after all, he was a pig, and protein is not a small thing here. Of course, Tay was devastated, she had thought Edgar was a permanent gift. It was quite pathetic really—she wrapped her arms around Edgar and wailed like a Banshee, screaming and crying. Nari and a few other villagers who had gathered were taken aback at first and then thought it was quite funny. Here was this little white girl with her arms entwined around a huge pig's neck crying like her life was ending. June and I talked about giving Nari some money for Edgar, but we decided that really wouldn't be the right thing to do. Anyway, Nari eventually led Edgar off with his bark-string leash, and June dragged Tay into the house and gave her a long talking to about how we were guests in Abini, that she wasn't a New Guinean, that she was embarrassing everyone, etc., etc.

Tay took off, as she often does when she is angry at June, and I didn't go to look for her immediately. When it got dark and she still wasn't back, I put on my boots, took an oil lantern, and checked the usual hiding places. No Taylor to be found. When I got back to the house, there was a man from Nari's hamlet waiting with June. It seems Tay was at his hamlet acting a bit strange, and it was dark anyway and they didn't want her roaming around Abini alone at night. When I got to the hamlet, there was a *mumu* in full swing (a *mumu* is an earth oven used to cook large quantities of food, and opening them and eating are mini-events that a whole hamlet partakes in).

It was quite a dramatic scene, really, with two bonfires going, illuminating the night, steamed greens, sweet potatoes, and pig meat spilling out of a hole in the ground, and everyone glowing in the firelight. And there was my daughter, squatting at the outer edge of the circle of feasting villagers, with a portion of food laid out on a banana leaf in front of her. The man who came to get me told me that Tay had come to the *mumu* because, as the pig's "mama," she knew she would be entitled to the best cut first. But, of course, Tay couldn't eat Edgar, and anyway I've warned her many, many times never to eat any pig meat prepared by the villagers because of trichinosis. So there she sat, filthy, tear streaked, and silent, watching the *mumu*.

I felt really sorry for her as we walked home in the dark. She wouldn't hold my hand, and after her bath June and I heard her sniffling in her bed. "It's okay, sweetie," June called out, and eventually the sounds from her room stopped.

I don't know, Mitch, I think it's nearing the time for us to pack up and leave the field. But I still have so much work to do here. I guess it's all about being able to live with yourself when you know you haven't accomplished what you set out to do and maybe you're not even so sure what that was in the first place.

Write soon,

Pete

EIGHT

Two weeks after his blood samples spoiled, Peter stopped doing fieldwork. He spent his days speaking Pisin with three Abini men who came to the compound in the morning and sat with him in the kitchen. He made coffee and stirred condensed milk into it and then poured each of them a full tin mug. The men sat on the floor and sipped the hot liquid while they rolled dry-store tobacco in newspaper and then smoked and talked until they could see the afternoon rains coming and left for their hamlets.

He began to go on trips with these men; at first it was only day-long hikes into the rain forest or a black cave that stretched the length of a mountain and housed thousands of bats. But eventually the trips became longer, and Peter would pack a small bag before he left and then spend several nights away from June and Taylor.

While he was up Mt. Orono, June stood on the rock in their compound and looked south, into the endless green distance, trying to see the mountain that Makino, Peter's friend, had pointed out to her.

When Peter got back, he told June that they had found mineral springs that bubbled out of the rocky summit. He said that the air was so thin at the peak of Mt. Orono that when he sat in the hot springs, naked, looking at the immense drop of the mountains below them, his nose bled for an hour.

And after the trip to Mt. Orono he told June that he was planning on going to a male initiation ceremony in Nilasa. He told her this after dinner, when they were drinking Chablis and listening to the BBC World Service's Philippines broadcast. Taylor was already sleeping, and the rain was loud on the fifty-gallon aluminum drum that stood outside of the kitchen, collecting water.

"Peter, do you really think it's the right thing? To stop working now?" June asked. "We've only been here seven months."

She didn't like being left alone in Abini. She couldn't sleep without Peter; the sounds outside the compound bothered her, and she had to leave on the two-way radio, which hiccuped static throughout the night.

"I can't do anything until the generator is working, anyway," he said. "And I want some time to elapse before we go out harvesting for blood again." He made a face. "The whole of Abini is going to think we're the most voracious vampires."

"When are you going?" she asked. Nilasa was an eighteen-hour walk from Abini, mostly through dense lowland rain forest, which meant two days on either side of the trip.

Peter shrugged. "Makino says the festivities start next week. I thought I'd take some photos."

"I see," June said. She poured some more Chablis into Peter's mug and then her own. "This is awful wine."

"Look, June, it's crazy to be here and not see the place. It's so, I don't know—unknown. It's exciting to be here—we're like explorers or something."

"The people here already know it plenty."

"Yeah, but they're unknown, too. Don't you see? I just think we should explore before we leave."

"We? You want to explore, I don't."

"Do you really hate it here so much, June?"

"No," she said. "But you could have asked me if I wanted to go to Nilasa." June glanced at Peter; with his burned red face and bleached hair, he looked as though he had spent a week at the beach. He wants to go alone, she thought, and she was nervous that he would get angry.

"Do you want to go? I thought you'd rather not."

"No, I don't really. I guess I just feel so alone when you take off for a mountaintop or something. You're getting like Taylor. Soon, I'm going to have to give you a disinfectant wash at the end of the day," she said and smiled.

Peter looked at her gravely. He reached his hand across the table and squeezed her fingers, but she let her hand lay limp in his. She looked at the Coleman lamp's bag glowing white and smiled.

···

That night June got into bed with her husband. She put her arm around his chest and then unbuttoned his pajama top. She slowly ran her fingertips across his skin, feeling the sparse chest hair and then the goose bumps she raised. Peter kissed the top of her head.

"June," he said. "What?"

June was silent. She reached over and put her mouth on his neck and breathed in his faint sour smell. It always amazed her that he hardly had any smell. He was clean and abbreviated even here in the field, while she was always full of odor—the deep musky smell from her vagina and armpits, the sweat on her skin.

His chest seemed to stretch forever, the muscles, the small pink nipples, the wideness of his body. When her hand dipped low, and she reached her fingers under the waistband into the curl of his pubic hair, he whispered, "June, I don't . . . I don't think I want to right now."

She pulled her hand up and rested it on his belly.

"It's not—I'm just not really wanting that right now." He paused and then breathed deeply.

"Are you ever going to want to again, Peter?"

"June," he said, and when he said her name like that, she wished she hadn't asked. "Yes, of course."

They were quiet then, and finally Peter said, "You're not upset?"

Somewhere in the corner of her mind she had been waiting for him to stop her.

"No," she said aloud, into the night, "I'm not upset."

She did not get out of the bed, though; she stayed there breathing him in, feeling his hair and face under her fingers. She could sense every part of his body as though it were her own—his toes with their dark, cracked nails, the stretch marks that covered his buttocks and thighs, his fingernails, his strong forearms covered in freckles and light brown hair. She reached down to touch his side; his skin was cool.

She stayed in bed with him, cramped, and as she drifted, hovering at the edge of sleep, feeling half-conscious nonsense thoughts circle in her mind, she was puzzled that she could not feel the chagrin that she saw so clearly in her soul.

. . .

When Peter left for Nilasa, June moved Taylor into his bed. Taylor and her doll Juliette and the two Raggedy Anns filled up the bedroom, and June was able to fall asleep soon after midnight.

With Peter gone the two of them were subdued. Taylor came back early from her visits to Beriapi, the hamlet where Nari and her children lived. For a few days, when Peter was first gone, she even stayed with her mother around the house. One morning they worked in the garden at the back end of the compound together. Taylor crouched next to her mother while she weeded and snipped basil and dill leaves and picked plum tomatoes off the vine. June pulled four carrots from the ground, snapping off the ends that had been chewed by rats and tossing them into the careful flood gutters that Peter had dug.

Taylor fed the chickens, spraying crumbs and cornmeal with her hands, addressing them all by name.

"How many have we got now?" June asked her.

Taylor thought for a moment. "Around twenty-six," she said.

"Have you named them all, funny girl?"

"Mom," she said. "Of course."

After lunch Taylor went off with Nari's daughters, and June was alone in the compound. Occasionally, one of the village women would bring her vegetables and stay for a while, but these visits were always awkward and, lately, infrequent. June did not even know the limited Abini vocabulary that Peter did, and the women could not (or would not, June often wondered) speak Pisin at all.

The cicadas were screaming, low and mild, and the sun was so strong it seemed to be adding to the day's sounds. June got *Tropic of Capricorn* and sat at the kitchen table with the window propped open, looking at Mt. Abini. She read for a while and then made herself a pot of coffee. It was so quiet. She realized that she liked it when it was like this—still and sunny, with everything in its place—

not rushing at her, forcing her to smell and feel and taste it. She drank the coffee and burned her lips on the metal rim of the cup and thought: I am waiting for Peter.

This is what she always did, wait for him to be present, to have an idea for them; and until he did she filled her time—killed her time—with distractions. June thought about Peter when she first met him, when they were both undergraduates in Cambridge. She had loved his long legs and too pretty features and his unconscious WASPy snobbery.

June had felt so ugly then—she could not believe that he was interested in her, not even when he pulled her to him outside of a restaurant and kissed her. When they slept together, she had been surprised at how thick and hairless his body was; he seemed almost like an athletic girl to her. He is so elusive, she thought, he has always been slipping away into thought. And she had loved that he wanted to be a scientist; she loved the way he cut his fingernails into short, neat squares and held her hand as he walked her through the laboratories and explained the impossible exotica of the equipment he used.

It wasn't fair that he didn't do well in graduate school—he wasn't political, she thought, he wasn't aggressive like the other grade-driven, jockeying, ambitious doctoral students at Harvard. June thought that he was like a nineteenth-century philosopher, full of passion for abstract connections. She sighed then and drank some of the lukewarm coffee that was sweet from the condensed milk. She couldn't do any work on the survey while Peter was gone or uninterested in it. She wouldn't know what needed to be done next, and the voluminous typed-up notes, photographs, and tape reels sealed in plastic bags in the office seemed inviolate. It had always been satisfying for her to bankroll their lives while Peter was in graduate school and now here in the field with the money her father left her.

She wanted Peter to start working again; she didn't like him when he wasn't working. He was moody and withdrawn and seemed to look at her with so much distance that it felt like contempt. She wondered where he was. Usually, when Peter was gone, she thought of him in a vague way of being in the same place, a realm where she didn't exist. But that afternoon she imagined him tromping through the rain forest, burning leeches off his legs with a cigarette, his canvas hat dark brown with sweat.

The morning he left for Nilasa June watched him get dressed through sleepy eyes. He pulled his socks up to his knees and wrapped a canteen around his waist with a green web belt.

"You look like a Boy Scout," she had said to him from the bed.

"Thanks a lot," he said and laughed, but she could hear that he was hurt.

After he left she couldn't sleep and had gone to the kitchen and looked at his breakfast dishes in the sink. She had been angry then, but now, looking out at the lazy, sunny day, she realized that she missed him, and in a general way that she was even worried about him. She shook her head and picked up her novel and read until Taylor came home, wet from the rains and hungry for afternoon tea.

...

It rained the entire way to Nilasa. The men from Abini walked up and down mountain ridges, through the forest, their legs and feet splattered with thick mud, with so much water in their eyes and mouths and ears that they could not talk or hear each other. Finally, Peter could not even think from the rain, and he only felt the water pounding on his head and body and the smell of the wet earth and the pepper scent of crushed leaves.

The rain stopped when they arrived at Nilasa. The sky over the village was still dark though, holding another storm in its wide, gray clouds. Peter and the men from Abini were staying in the long, rectangular men's house, which stood at the back of Nilasa's main hamlet. Makino had explained that this was the only way to be safe from poison men when they were on enemy soil—they could not possibly be attacked in so public a place.

Peter was disappointed. He would have preferred to stay in the patrol officer's hut, where he could hang his lantern from a hook and read and write and sketch and sleep in quiet. He thought about getting Makino to ask the Nilasa men if he could stay alone in the *kiap*'s hut, but he was too tired to make a fuss, and he shrugged his shoulders and walked up the flimsy stairs into the *haus man*.

The initiates, they could not be older than twelve or thirteen, he thought, were huddled by the doorway, covered in red grease and black feather headdresses, dozing and whispering to each other. Peter was too tall for the long house, and he bent his head as he passed the boys and walked to an empty area behind the second fire pit. He spread out his damp sleeping bag and pulled his plastic-bagged Nikon, light meter, flashes, and canisters of film out of his rucksack, nervous that the equipment was ruined. He lay down then and fell asleep in the crowded, smoke-filled space while the men around him prepared for the initiation. When he surfaced into semi-consciousness, he felt the exhaustion in his spine and blood from the walk and the endless rain.

Finally, the noise of men talking and singing woke him up. He walked outside and pissed behind the pig fence that ringed the hamlet and filled his lungs with cold, fresh Highlands air and shook his head. He didn't feel right—he was still fatigued, and hungry now, as well. How long had he been in Nilasa? He looked at his watch, and the date suddenly seemed absurd to him. Why was the Western world obsessed with numbering and tracking time, he wondered. It was so silly. The idea of hours and dates and years seemed pointless to him then, and he reached his hand up to his forehead and felt how hot he was. Time is wide, he thought; he had come all the way to this place to be able to see that. It was not narrow and long the way they pretended in America.

An intense dizzy feeling spread through his body, and he leaned against the *haus man* for support. He stood up straight and walked back inside, taking in the expressions on the faces of the men and the boys in the firelight, who were staring at him—with what? curiosity? anger? I must look ridiculous, he thought. He saw Makino sitting by his equipment, and he laughed. I am ridiculous, he thought. How absurd it is that I am here.

And then, later that night in the *haus man,* a few hours before dawn, the initiates, their skin gleaming with dyed-red pig's fat, were shown the flutes. Peter was wide awake, excited, and feverish. When the initiates, who were exhausted from being kept up for four days in the smoke-filled, dark, crowded house, saw the flutes, they began to cry. Were they just exhausted, Peter wondered. Or furious to have been prodded awake, terrified, abused, all to be shown decorated bamboo tubes at the climax? Or did these flutes move them that much? The initiates looked away from the flutes, and the men who had presented them put them down and casually began to roll cigarettes and scratch the sleep out of their eyes.

Soon they started singing to the initiates, a dissonant, moaning, quiet song that filled the silence and was accompanied only by the crackling of dry wood burning in the fire pit. At dawn cooked, cold sweet potatoes were passed around. Peter was starving, and he gulped his down in big swallows, noting the haunted look in the boys' faces. As far as he could tell, the initiates had eaten nothing and been given only small sips of water for the past four days. He ate a second potato and then greedily chewed into a section of sugar cane, sucking the sweet juice from the bark with a loud sound.

He knew he was sick. He could feel an ache growing above his belly and a fever, although he wasn't sure how distorted his sense of temperature was from the immense heat in the *haus man*.

"*Mi kisim sik,*" he said to Makino, who was sitting next to him. Makino looked at him and clucked his tongue.

"*Ai, sori,*" Makino said and then turned his face back to the initiates.

They are always this way, Peter thought; illness is a nuisance to them, like missing a train or getting locked out of the apartment is for me. Thinking of home made him sad, and he wished that he could take Makino to Boston and show him the city, his apartment, how there were so many houses, so many people in Cambridge, and the wide, dirty Charles. He thought of June, and he was confused—was she waiting for him in Boston, or was she there in New Guinea with him? But he knew that she was in Abini, and he could see her face, and her fingers, and the smooth skin on her neck, and he thought: I don't love her. The thought shocked him and seemed cruel, and he shook his head to get rid of it.

Peter felt the sweat on his neck and back and underarms. The smoke from the fire was making his eyes water, and he stroked his eyelashes with his fingertips.

The men pulled out old, dirt-encrusted razor blades and began cutting the boys on their legs and necks and under their nipples. They gathered the blood that was bright red even in the dull, smoke-filled room, in banana-leaf cups and then tied them into balls and hung them over the fire. The men began singing again, and Peter wished that Taylor were there to tell him what the songs were about. He had noticed though, that when Makino or someone else summarized what had been said, it was often different from Taylor's translation, either because she did not understand the language as well as he thought she did or because translating bored her and she did it sloppily.

He closed his eyes and felt an enormous exhaustion well up in him. He could not remember ever being this tired, and he knew he was slipping out of consciousness. When he woke up, he did not know where he was, and the red, grease-covered boys and the men chattering and shouting in Abini began to blend into a dark pattern where he could no longer make out individuals. The men started to play bamboo flutes, and the sound disappointed Peter. The flutes sounded distant and reedy, and the music had no melody, only an insistent percussive drive. He looked around the room and tried to find Makino or any of the other men he had come from Abini with, but he could not distinguish any of the people around him.

It was only when he saw Taylor, sitting near the door with poinsettia leaves crowning her head, that he realized he was hallucinating. Ah, he thought, I am really very sick now. And then he was aware of fainting into Makino's arms.

...

Peter was carried back from Nilasa on a stretcher made out of two baru trees lashed together with vines and a dried pandanas leaf mat. It took the men he was with three days to carry him to Abini. On the uphill hike back they had sheltered him from the rains with banana leaves and cleaned him when he vomited and urinated and defecated on the stretcher. When they brought him into the compound, he stank, and the yellow in his eyeballs and skin terrified June. A young boy who had walked from Nilasa handed June Peter's canvas bag, bulky with his camera, notebook, and empty canteen. The bag was dirty and smelled like smoke. June held it to her stomach as she followed the men carrying Peter into the house. She did not want to be alone in the house with her husband so sick, and she made a pot of coffee for the men and put a tin of Danish butter cookies on the table.

While Peter's companions talked quietly in the kitchen, June gave him a sponge bath. As she dipped the blue washcloth into a tin bowl of hot water and Phisoderm, she wanted to shake him awake and say, See, you need a disinfectant wash now, like Taylor. But he was unconscious as she wiped the cloth along his chest and abdomen and listened to the men who brought him home walk out of their house.

Taylor helped her mother get Peter into his sleeping bag, and the two of them stood at his side, looking at him.

"What does he have, Mom?" Taylor asked.

"I think he has hepatitis," June said. She pushed her hair back from her forehead. The *kiaps* who came through Abini talked to them about Nilasa and the rest of the lowlands as if they were leper colonies, with malaria, typhoid fever, and virulent hepatitis lurking in the hamlets. He knew, June thought. This is all on purpose.

...

The next morning when Peter became conscious, June fed him watery chicken broth made from a bouillon cube and spooned sweet, milky Earl Grey into his mouth.

"Where's Tay?" he asked.

"She's outside, playing. Your yellow eyes scare her. She thinks you look like a *kore bana*," June said.

Peter smiled. "I feel like one. God, I'm really sick, June," he said.

"No, you're not, come on," she said.

"This wasn't part of the deal, was it?"

"I don't know," she said. "What was the deal, Peter?"

"I'm sorry," he said.

"Peter," June said, "you're not that sick."

"I want to talk, June," he said. "Let's really talk."

"Later," she said. "When you're feeling better."

"I'm feeling better now," he said.

June picked up the soup bowl and the mug of tea and walked out of the bedroom. She did not want to hear what he had figured out in Nilasa after she had missed him so much now that he was here, jaundiced and full of fever, bursting with self-realization.

"June," he called her in a weak voice.

She gathered her hair into an elastic and walked by the bedroom door to the two-way radio in their office. She picked up the handset and started to call the British Medical Institute. She sat there listening to the static, and the high-pitched voice of the missionary in Kainantu, and the distant sounds of Motu. And finally, she listened to her own voice with its modulated and clear American accent, echoing back through the radio's speakers: "Abini—Goroka. Abini—Goroka. Come in, please."

...

June sat on her bed and watched Peter sleep. When he drifted back to her, drowsy in his fever, he talked only of dying. He rambled on, outlining plans for her to implement when he died: how she would handle his corpse, what she would say in Port Moresby to the American consulate, where she would stop in Australia. She knew that people did not die of hepatitis A, and she tried at first to comfort him, but when she could not stop the rush of detailed instructions for his funeral and where to send Taylor to school, she had screamed at him.

"Stop it," he had said, all of a sudden alert and serious. "You'll frighten Taylor."

"*I'll* frighten Taylor?"

And then Peter had smiled and closed his eyes, murmuring something—was it about her? His voice trailed off, and he went back to sleep.

June radioed the British Medical Institute every morning with the minutiae of Peter's condition. Sometimes she spoke with

Fitzroy and sometimes with Dennis, his South African assistant. She realized when she spoke to them how lonely she was. When Dennis told her that her mother had called them, concerned about her, she had taken her fingers off the radio handset and wept. They told her that there was nothing to do for Peter; he must sleep and drink fluids.

"He's stopped doing fieldwork," she told Fitzroy over the radio.

"Yes, well, he's got hepatitis. I'd say under the circumstances that's fairly reasonable."

June wanted to tell him the truth, that Peter had stopped working before he got sick, that he did not care about the research anymore, that he spent his time going to the rain forest and talking to the village men. But instead she only said: "I'm frightened."

"Of course you are, June, that's natural," he said, "but it seems worse than it is. This will ultimately be another exploit you'll regale your friends with."

She was shocked then. She put down the handset and walked into the kitchen to fill up the kettle for Taylor's bath. She had forgotten that she would ever leave Abini.

NINE

Roy Urqhartt did fieldwork in the Joa valley for two years before he grew his beard Highlands style and married a village woman. After the news of his wedding feast (for which he stripped naked and covered himself in the traditional red grease of a Joa groom) traveled to town, most of the whites in Goroka avoided him. There had been an unpleasant scene once, when he came out of the field and tried to stay at the Lutheran guest house with his Joa wife, so now he made his forays for resupply alone, buying groceries at Steamships and drinking at the Bird of Paradise with the *kiaps,* filling the bar with his loud Scottish brogue.

On this trip the anthropologist had rented the British Medical Institute's visiting-scientist room and spent three uncomfortable nights there. When his shopping and drinking were finally done, he booked a flight back to Joa on the Christ Church Mission's Cessna. He was irked that morning when he got to the Goroka airstrip and Keith London, the pilot, told him that they were stopping in Abini and at a mission in Moimanu before Joa. Roy, sullen and still half asleep, helped Keith pack his supplies and knapsack into the back of the small plane.

A few bored-looking New Guinean men leaned against the mission flight shack and watched the plane buzz down the dirt runway and then take off. As they headed up into the morning mist, Roy contemplated Goroka-town disappearing from view with satisfaction. Soon they passed over the new government buildings at Lufa station that were arranged in neat box formation, carefully fenced in from the road. A lonely white Nissan was driving east out of Lufa, and Roy watched it amble along the rain-pocked Highlands highway. Being in Goroka put Roy into a bad mood, and as he saw the mountains below him become steep and covered in dense, blue-green rain forest, he felt better.

Fifteen minutes after they passed Lufa station, the Campbells' compound appeared on the horizon, in the shadow of Mt. Philip. Their house was wide, covered by a striped roof of corrugated aluminum, green fiberglass, and thatch. An open-walled shed at the edge of the compound housed a generator, a Honda motorbike, and a fifty-gallon water tank. Americans, Roy thought. So much bloody money and no fucking sense. He had heard both Campbells on the radio speaking to Tony Fitzroy, sending their flat American voices across the Eastern Highlands. He knew a few things about them: their daughter had been sick, the woman's mother called Goroka from the States constantly and demanded that her messages be relayed, and the man was sick now, too.

Roy was the closest white person to them—Joa was only a fourteen-hour walk from Abini, but the anthropologist had resisted radioing over to them and introducing himself in the usual whites-in-the-bush-stick-together fashion. He didn't like Americans, and after listening to their radio calls, these ones in particular struck him as foolish. Keith circled the airstrip twice looking for a path through the thick clouds. Finally, he brought the Cessna down.

"We're only here for a moment, mate," Keith said while the propeller slowed.

"Good," Roy said.

"Y'comin out? Might want to be neighborly, eh?" Keith asked as he pulled his seat back and grabbed the Campbells' boxes of groceries and mail.

"All right," he said. "All right."

Roy looked out at the faces of the Abini villagers who had gathered to meet the plane—it was everyone who wasn't far away in a garden, he'd bet. He pushed open the door and lit a cigarette. He sat there smoking, letting them watch him while he looked out at the airstrip. He was white and from Joa—too much, he thought. They'll worry about poison. He stroked his beard and drew in on the cigarette and then exhaled, filling the inside of the Cessna with smoke.

He scanned the crowd until he saw the Big Man. Roy got out of the plane then and walked straight toward him. The Big Man was easy for him to pick out—pastel-colored plastic bracelets encircled his upper arms, a dirty canvas hat sat low on his forehead, and he was skinny, wearing a loincloth and a tanket-leaf covering over his buttocks. His face was beautiful, Roy thought, although he was old now, wrinkled, and his teeth had fallen out, but his intelligence was bright and obvious.

"*Mornin,*" Roy said and offered him a cigarette.

The Abini Big Man took the cigarette and smiled. The villagers who crowded around the two of them looked pleased. He had got it right, and they were relieved. The Big Man didn't know Pisin, or he wouldn't admit to it, and so Roy talked with a younger man who nodded and laughed and translated their conversation into a rapid stream of *tok ples* after each phrase Roy uttered. After a while they stopped talking and stood there, comfortably smoking as they felt the day become stronger on their skin.

"*Olrait,*" he said, "*mi bai go lukim misses.*"

They expected that, too. They would think it was strange verging on scandalous if he didn't talk to the American woman at the edge of the airstrip.

Roy walked across the sparse grass, and a group of children followed him, giggling and pushing each other as he approached the crowd that surrounded June Campbell and her boxes. She was bent over, and a green bandanna was pulled tight around her hair.

"Hullo!" he shouted to her.

She looked up at him, and he was amazed by her deep brown eyes and the serious expression on her face. She was tired, he could see that, but she was present, too, taking in everything around her. And her skin—she was so pale, untouched by the intimate mountain sun. How could a person stay that white up here at twelve thousand feet?

"Good morning," she said and bent back down over her box. She was checking the bags of rice, cereal, chocolate bars, the tins of duck and fruit cake, making sure that whoever she had told her shopping list to had been careful with it. She was being rude, he realized, and in that moment, he liked her.

"I'm Roy Urqhartt," he said.

"Yes," she said. "And I'm June Campbell."

He stood there waiting for her to stand up and shake his hand and talk to him. He couldn't believe that she wasn't hungry to speak English with him, that she wouldn't try to delay him and Keith and ask them in for tea, the way whites in the bush, especially whites with sick spouses, always did. But instead she moved over to the second box and began checking its contents in her methodical manner. Roy imagined her in civilization, her lovely white skin bared by an expensive dress, sheer stockings on her legs, her black hair curled, with the same disdainful manner about her. He got nervous then and almost laughed out loud at the vision.

"How's your husband?" he asked.

"Bad," she said and looked back at him at last. "He got hepatitis in Nilasa."

"Did he?" Roy asked.

"We're just right," she said, and Roy realized that she was talking about her groceries. *"Tokim tenk yu tru lon Masta Balus,"* she said and sent a boy running to thank Keith, who was back at the Cessna already.

"Are you going to fly your husband out?" Roy asked.

"No," she said, "the worst of it's over. He's as happy to recuperate here as he would be in Goroka."

"I see," he said. He glanced past June and saw their house through the trees. He thought about offering to keep in touch, or to help her, but how could he? Instinctively, he stayed quiet. He did not want to get involved with these people. He felt how protective, how secretive she was—of what? Her family? Her husband?

"Where's your daughter?" he asked.

June looked at him, and Roy was again taken aback by the intensity of her gaze. She was certainly attractive, he thought, not beautiful but compelling. Unconsciously, he shook his head and touched the soft bottom of his beard. He watched her breathe out a heavy sigh and put her hand to her hip. Ah, he thought, she's suffering here. He had an urge to make her talk about her life, to put his fingers on her face.

Keith shouted, "Right, Urqhartt, we've got to get going," to him from the Cessna.

"She's at the gardens," June said. "The groceries arriving aren't so very exciting for her."

Roy nodded and looked up at the group of children standing near the plane. He wanted to keep talking to June, but she wouldn't walk him to the Cessna even if he asked her to. The clouds were thinning and the sky was pure blue, like springtime in a dream. He could feel the sun-warmed air pouring into the surrounding rain forest. He tried to think of something to say to her—he felt sure he wouldn't see her again, and it made him sad. But all he came up with was: "We're going to the Christ Mission up in Moimanu now. Keith's got mail and things for them, too."

June nodded, distracted. He was already gone for her. She called out to two boys to carry the boxes back to the compound.

"Very well then," she said. "Nice to see you."

He turned away, and he felt her watch him. She had to stay at the airstrip until the Cessna took off and disappeared from view because none of the villagers (especially not the little boys she hired to carry for her) would miss the excitement of the plane's engine roaring to life, its wobbly taxi down the airstrip, and then its ascent into the clouds.

"She's a strange bird," Roy said to Keith when he had pulled the belt across his chest and slipped it into its buckle between his legs.

"Y'reckon?" Keith asked. "Seems all right to me." And he sat staring at his controls as he readied the plane for takeoff.

He thinks *I'm* one to talk, Roy reasoned. He knew the *kiaps* and pilots like Keith who had been to Joa were disgusted by the way he lived. "You stink of *kanaka*, Roy, *yu go was was*," a pilot had laughed at him one night when he was drinking in the Bird. And even though Roy had guessed what they must think of him, he had been mortified to hear it and to see the drunken smirks that confronted him from around the bar.

You're an ignorant bastard, Keith, Roy thought, and then got angry with himself for wanting so much to talk about June that he attempted to converse with this Australian ape who didn't even like him. He looked out the plane's window and tried to see June walking down the path to her house with the two boys behind her, but they were already too high up in the sky; even the Abini airstrip was barely visible.

Roy sat there next to Keith, contemplating the rain forest that was full of thick rivers and waterfalls and every once in a while an enormous kitchen garden. And then he began to think about June Campbell again: it's always like that with whites in the bush, he thought—it's the lady missionary and the anthropologist's wife who do the real coping, the blood, shit, and sweat level of interacting. It's white women, not men, who might possibly get something out of being here, besides leeches and malaria, and most of them are bloody frightened fools and impose their limited little outlooks on the world around them. It's too hard for her, though, she's too much there—she's spinning and spinning and watching, and she doesn't really understand it, maybe just a second or two of insight every few weeks. But she sees things, at least. The *kiaps,* some of them, come close, but they're just in and out, they never stay, they never live there and feel it, like the way that woman is feeling it. They're tough, though. She's not tough. She's lonely, too, probably doesn't like anyone anymore.

Keith flew around Mt. Philip and then northeast out of the Abini valley. In ten minutes they were over the Christ Mission's compound with its white-painted schoolhouse and muddy soccer field spread out in front. The missionary's converts had planted a large cross out of pink and red impatiens on the ground, and tired-looking chickens pecking at the flowers were visible from the air.

As Keith brought the Cessna around for descent, Roy looked at the villagers waiting by the side of the Moimanu airstrip, impatient for them to land.

TEN

When June opened her eyes, it was dark and she was afraid. She had been pulled out of sleep by the sound of the bamboo walls being slapped and insistent, hushed voices speaking Abini. She looked at Peter's clock. The luminescent dial read four-thirty; it was earlier than the villagers ever came to the compound.

"Peter," she hissed, "do you hear that?"

But her husband lay still on his bed, breathing shallow, loud breaths into the air.

June put her bathrobe over her pajamas and slipped on her mud-encrusted boots at the back door. When she walked outside, the cold, gray-blue dawn shocked her. The trees surrounding the compound were full of clouds, and steam was rising in slow columns from the ground. She could feel the darkness ebbing, wistfully leaving the landscape. Across the valley smoke was seeping through thatch roofs in Beriapi, and she saw an orange flash of a cooking fire and a figure walk inside a hut.

She turned and saw Nari standing with her two daughters and teenage son close to the front door.

"*Wannim samtin?*" she asked. She could tell that they had been watching her, silently, since she came outside. Nari's husband, Tinu, appeared from around the side of the house. He was wearing a loin-cloth and a green T-shirt with "Tooranga Park" written across it in faded white lettering. He walked close to her, holding several 20 kina notes in his hand.

"Misses," he said. "*Mori em givem dispela lon pikinini.*"

June shook her head. She did not know what he meant, or why he was there so early with his family.

"*Mori em givem,*" he repeated. Mori—with a rush June understood. Mori was their name for Taylor.

"*Wannim?*" she asked. Tinu told her that Taylor had given his children three 20 kina notes, and he had discovered the money hidden in his house the night before. He held out the cash to her.

As soon as she took it from his hand, Tinu lunged for his son. He smacked the boy in the face and then hit him in the back so forcefully that the boy dropped to his knees and started to cry loud sobs in a hoarse adolescent voice. Tinu then pulled the two girls by their ears and hit both of them in the face.

"*Maski!*" June cried. Stop.

But Tinu did not listen to her, and Nari stood watching her husband beating her children. The three children began to howl, and the boy put his hands up to his face to shield himself from his father's blows. June wanted to run inside, but she knew she had to stay—she realized that this was being done for her.

Tinu began to yell in Pisin: *"Yu no inap stealman moni bilon wait man."* You can't steal the white man's money. The two girls were huddled next to each other, sobbing.

June said to Nari in Pisin, "I'm sorry," and then to Tinu: "Can you translate that for her?"

Tinu looked over at June. She felt as though the money in her hands was burning, hot and bright.

"Meri save pisin," he said. The woman knows Pisin.

Tinu and Nari turned from her and walked away, talking together in the still darkness. When they got to the compound's fence, their children stood up and ran after them. June was alone then, watching the dawn turn into morning.

...

June walked into Taylor's bedroom holding the money Tinu had given her. Taylor was sitting up in the cot, hugging her sleeping bag to her chest.

"You took Daddy's money from his wallet while he was sick," she said, "and gave it to your friends."

Taylor looked at the floor. It seemed to June that her daughter had willed herself to become a solid mass without a soul, completely still and emotionless. June felt like hitting her. Taylor looked up, and her blue eyes were flat.

"Do you think those children thought it was your money?" she asked.

She is just a girl, June told herself. She does not know what she does. But she did not really believe it. It disgusted her that Taylor hid so much from her. She is not like a child, she thought; she never has been.

"Well?" she asked. She could see that Taylor was deciding something.

"Are you going to tell Daddy?"

"Of course, Taylor. Daddy and I talk about everything." June paused. "We talk about every single thing." She spoke slowly, emphasizing the syllables, so the words came out: ev-ery sing-el thingah.

"Daddy is very upset about you, and now this." June shook her head. She wanted to make sure that Taylor understood that Peter didn't sympathize with her. She wanted Taylor to see that she and Peter were the same. "I'm going to go talk about your punishment with him right now. You heard what happened to your friends."

For the first time that morning June saw an emotion on Taylor's face. She could not tell what her daughter was feeling at first. But as she walked out of Taylor's room down the hall, she realized that what she had seen circle up and around the girl until it spread across the features of her face was hatred.

...

June didn't hear Taylor leave that morning, but she knew the girl was gone. She sat in the bedroom feeding Peter soup she made out of beef bouillon and boiled cabbage, and she thought about Taylor hiding, waiting for June to come and find her. She had told Peter the story about Tinu and the money. He seemed to regret that he had missed it, and he made her recount the episode in detail.

"Where's Taylor now?" he asked.

"Off somewhere being pissy," she said. June had made a pitcher of Tang, and she poured some into a tin mug and handed it to him.

"Could you open the window?" he asked.

June leaned over Peter's bed and pushed open the window. They both looked out at the bright afternoon and the green of Mt. Abini in the distance.

"You should go look for her soon," Peter said.

"She'll be back later," June said. "I'm not humoring this."

"She gets into trouble on her own."

June sighed. "I don't understand you. You said she should be free to roam, that you didn't think the allergy stuff was going to happen again. And now I'm supposed to take care of you and chase after her every time she gets her nose out of joint?"

"I said I couldn't believe that it would happen again."

"What she did, with the money, that whole thing this morning, was outrageous."

Peter was quiet. "She didn't mean for that to happen. I understand that. She was trying to be nice."

"Really? I think she was showing off. She doesn't realize the effect that she has here."

"Come on," Peter said. "You should hear how harsh you sound."

"She runs away so we'll follow her. It's all about attention." At that moment June had a fantasy that Taylor was under the house, listening to her and Peter, and it made her angrier at both of them.

"I still think you should go look for her before the rain starts. You don't want to make her sulk in the rain."

"Jesus Christ," June said. "Really."

. . .

By the time the afternoon rain clouds were rolling in over the mountains, blocking the view from the compound with their dark gray fullness, Peter was in a fever. June gave him an alcohol rub, pulling wet cotton balls across his chest and then along his neck and forehead. She hated it when he got so sick; she felt as though he were dead and she was alone in the room with his jaundiced, skinny corpse. He mumbled to her then, and she patted his hand and looked out the window: the dark was pouring in and the cicadas were screaming warning about the rains.

June walked outside and stood on the rock at the end of the compound.

"Okay, Taylor, you win. You can come in now," she shouted. "Just come in before the rain starts. Daddy's worried."

June got down from the rock and walked over to the chicken coop and looked around it. She went into their garden and peered into the ditches that were shielded by the wide, flowering squash plants and Peter's carefully staked tomatoes. She stood with her hands on her hips. She checked behind the bamboo stand at the north end of the compound and then climbed over the fence and walked down to the road.

She saw a young man walking toward her. His wife was following him, and she was bent under an enormous net bag filled with sweet potato, cut sugar cane sections, greens, and firewood. The woman looked up and smiled at June. June asked the man— had he seen Taylor, or heard of her being anywhere? He shook his head and pointed to the rain clouds: they had been in the garden all day, he said, and were hurrying home now to avoid the rains.

June thanked them and began walking quickly up the path that led from the road to Beriapi. She stuck her head into one of the huts that was near the hamlet's entrance, and she was overwhelmed by the smoke and the smell of pig excrement. An old woman sitting by the fire, tending sweet potatoes in the ashes, shook her head. Her son, who stood up when he saw June at the door, said that they hadn't seen Taylor since the day before. The woman took a torch, made from lashed-together wild sugar cane, from the rafters and pressed its head into her fire and then handed it to June. The old woman's torch burned out by the time she got to the compound fence, and she threw the blackened pieces into a ditch.

Standing there, in the dark, at the edge of the compound, she thought about how it would be when she got inside the house and Peter asked about Taylor. How had the girl turned everything around so that she could manipulate her mother and father? The thought came into her being that Peter liked his daughter more than he liked her. He enjoyed Taylor, he liked watching her run off into the mountains with her friends. And then the rain came—for a second it was light, gentle, and then it began to pour with all its force, pelting her, pushing into her eyes and ears and lips. June ran up the stairs into the back door, and without taking her boots off, she looked in Taylor's room, in the kitchen, and in the front of the house.

She lit the Coleman and boiled water for rice and heated up a tin of curried duck. She checked in the bedroom and saw that Peter was sleeping. She ate and then made a plate for Taylor and put it inside the oven. When the rain stopped, she took an oil lamp and stood on the back steps, but she could not see beyond the flame's shallow glow. There was only a sliver of a moon, and the dark was pure black and thick. It was cold, and the girl would be wet and sad. Come on, daughter, she thought, give in.

She walked down the stairs and held the lamp under the house. All day she had secretly thought that Taylor was under the house. She had refused to look there, compromising with her in her mind: if you are close to home, I won't bother you. She walked under the house then, crouched over, and held the lamp up above her head, illuminating the earth floor. Her daughter was not there. When June realized that Taylor was really nowhere near, for the first time that day she felt the enormity of her daughter's unforgiving fury.

...

In the morning June walked over to Beriapi and asked a group of men sitting in the grove of coffee trees that framed the hamlet's entrance if one of them would help her find Taylor. A young man, Jaru, who had gone to Nilasa with Peter, stood up and agreed to come with her. As they walked back to the compound, June told him that she would pay him. Jaru shrugged his shoulders. He waited for her, squatting on the lawn in front of the house, while she went inside and ate a cheese sandwich and drank a pot of coffee.

June put on khaki pants and a long-sleeve cotton shirt. She rubbed zinc oxide cream on her face and hands and then put on her wide-brimmed bush hat. She strapped Peter's watch on her wrist and packed a small canvas bag with a canteen, some Band-Aids, a pocket knife, folded toilet paper, insect repellent, the tube of zinc oxide, and two Cadbury bars. She swung the bag over her shoulder and nestled it by her hip.

When she came outside, Jaru offered to carry her bag for her, but she shook her head no. They walked out of the compound, past Beriapi, east on the road that led to the next village, Malvi. The cold of morning was still in the air, and the route was familiar to June. She and Peter had walked it every morning when they were surveying the hamlets of Abini. As they passed these hamlets, Jaru would climb the fences and ask if anyone had seen Taylor.

A group of children followed them for a while, giggling and calling out, *"Mornin, misses,"* to her. When June answered them, they would laugh and whisper, and a few of the smaller girls ran next to her and held her hand. As noon approached, the children turned back, and the sun burned through the clouds. June began sweating. The zinc ran into her eyes and she stopped and took a piece of toilet paper from her bag and rubbed her eyelids with it and then wiped the rest of the cream off her face.

The road narrowed until it became a path when they passed the last hamlet in Abini. She had never walked beyond this point with Peter, and she asked Jaru then if he thought Taylor would have gone this far. Jaru looked at her and then out at the path, which was framed by a pig fence and overgrown wild sugar cane.

"I don't know," he said in Pisin. "She could have."

June nodded her head. She walked behind Jaru, trying to mimic his agile leaps over puddles and logs submerged in the muddy ground. She kept up with him for a few minutes, but eventually she slowed down and was alone in the corridor of wild sugar cane. The sun was hot, and as it dried the muddy path, the smell of wet earth and pig excrement was strong. The greenery gave way, and the path veered around a garden, up the slope of a hill. She could see Jaru ahead of her, sitting under a tree, smoking.

The garden was newly planted: sweet potato cuttings sat in bald lumps of earth looking dried out, and thin sugar cane plantings were lashed to wood sticks. A black layer of ash still covered the earth from when the forest had been cut and burned away for the planting. I am playing Taylor's game, June thought, the girl is no-where near this place; she is hidden, safe, in a fold of the valley, or in a hut in Beriapi, concealed from me by a loyal friend.

When June reached Jaru, she pulled her canteen from the bag and took two sips of the warm, tinny-tasting water. They started walking again, past the garden, through a grove of coffee trees where the path widened again. After a while the path was interrupted by a hamlet, and as June followed Jaru and climbed over the fence, she thought it was deserted. A fat black pig was sleeping under a boarded-up dry store, and they could hear the distant sound of someone singing out across the valley. As they reached the far fence of the hamlet, they came upon a woman laying her shelled coffee beans out on a dried pandanas-leaf mat. The woman looked up at Jaru and then over at June. She seemed unsurprised to see a white woman appear in her hamlet in the middle of the day.

Jaru spoke to her in Abini, and the woman shook her head and began smoothing the tan-colored beans with her palms. A little boy, naked except for a tattered cloth sash that had been tied around his distended belly, looked out of the hut. When he saw June, he began to scream, shrieking and crying tears down his face. Without turning, the woman shouted at the child, and June recognized two words of the woman's tirade: *kore bathaha*. Ghost woman. It incensed her that this woman told her child that she was a ghost. She smiled at the boy, who began screaming louder.

"She's scaring the baby," June said to Jaru.

He nodded, and as they left the hamlet, he said, "She told the child that you came here to eat it."

The path became wide again, and June and Jaru passed people who looked at June with muted surprise. She wondered why they were so incurious; none of them greeted her or smiled or came to touch her the way people in Abini had when she first arrived there. Jaru stopped and uttered a brief greeting and a few words in Abini with the people on the road. June wondered if he was still asking about Taylor, or did he think that this trip was a whim of hers? It was terrible that she couldn't speak Abini, and she forced herself to listen to Jaru, to try to distinguish words that might be familiar. She looked at his face, but he seemed relaxed and guileless.

Jaru walked off the road and cut down a tree sapling with his machete. He skinned the bark and sliced off the little branches. He handed it to her and said it would help her keep steady. June looked at the walking stick and shook her head. The road was wide and easy to walk on. She told him she didn't want it. Jaru threw the stick over the trees into the bushes.

"You'll want it later," he said.

"I'll ask you for it later," she said peevishly.

The road narrowed again. They passed two hamlets that looked strange to June. The huts with little patches of taro gardens behind them were different than the ones in Abini. The people who came to the doors of their houses nodded but did not come out to greet her. They seemed hostile, and she remembered then that Craig Michaels had told her and Peter that the Australians had come here and put down intense and vicious warfare that went on between Malvi and Abini.

She looked at Jaru and wondered if he were nervous, but he only stared straight ahead. She had no idea how old he was. Could he remember the warring? Or was it only stories to him? They stopped under a wide pine tree, and June took out a Cadbury bar. She opened the tinfoil and licked the melted, thick chocolate. Jaru ate a cooked sweet potato. He pointed at where they had come from, and she saw Mt. Abini and Mt. Philip in the distance. They were far away. Her shirt was wet with sweat, and her hair was damp against her scalp. She could feel that her face was burning—the hat's brim wasn't enough to shield her from the intensity of the afternoon equatorial sun. Mad dogs and Englishmen go out in the midday sun, she thought, and laughed out loud.

"Wannim?" Jaru asked her.

She tried to think of a way to translate the phrase. "Only crazy white people like to walk in the sun," she said in Pisin.

Jaru nodded. She watched him roll a cigarette, tearing small pieces off a chunk of braided tobacco and then carefully arranging it in yellowed newsprint. She knew they weren't going to find Taylor. Disheartened, she watched Jaru smoke and then looked up at the cloudless, too blue sky and back at the orange earth road.

"I don't think the girl is this way," Jaru said.

She knew he was right, and she wanted to turn around. The smell and heat and landscape that was flattening out the farther east they walked from Abini made her uncomfortable and uneasy. But she shook her head. "I want to go farther," she said. As she heard the Pisin words come out of her mouth, she was vaguely surprised, although she knew she meant them.

When they had got beyond the hamlets of Malvi, the road became a path again, and they entered a light, regrowth rain forest. Jaru told her that there was a huge garden that some Abini and Malvi women, who were in-laws, shared. He told her that Taylor had been to this garden, named Ikinibi, and that it had two rain shelters that were as big as houses.

"Maybe," Jaru said, "she's there."

The regrowth forest shielded them from the sun, and all of a sudden the air was green and cool. They walked along enormous felled tree trunks that were laid out one after the other as a path. June heard the harsh caw caw of a raggiana over the lighter web of bird calls. She took off her hat and put it in her bag. She thought about leeches and rolled her pants into tight cuffs so that she could see her sock-covered ankles as she walked.

The forest cleared away then, and June could see Ikinibi's pig fence in the distance. The sun hit them again with its full force, and June shielded her eyes with her hand. When she climbed over the fence and stood at the edge of the garden, she stared in disbelief. Ikinibi was enormous—larger than any garden she had ever seen, or imagined. It seemed to stretch forever, over the mountain, to the horizon line. She could see a river that flowed through its far end, its swollen banks surrounded by banana trees and cardamom bushes.

She was awed by the size and the exquisite rush of greens, yellows, and purples that covered the slope. The garden was silent; only the river's rushing water made any noise. She saw a yellow and black spider lazily crawling up the web it had spun over a sweet potato plant.

June dropped her hand from her eyes, and the intense sunlight in her pupils momentarily covered the landscape in a blue wash. And then, when the true colors came back, her soul was soaring in the air, high toward the sun, up above the sweet potato ivy–covered slopes of Ikinibi. She could see the river, split at the summit, crashing down through the garden and down the heavily forested backside of the mountain, carving its rocky bed.

She felt ecstatic then, and wild with the place, and looked over past a grove of banana trees to the pandanas's red fruits that hung from their boughs like phalluses. She thought of the story of the flutes that she had heard from an anthropologist in Goroka. She closed her eyes and saw that perfect moment when the men had played the flutes and filled the canopy with their deep thud-thud music for a man they thought was their ancestor, made into a terrible god and returned to them.

She opened her eyes, and they were radiant with the day and the fast flow of her emotions. Her arms and legs were trembling, and she looked at Jaru. She wanted to cry out then, and make a sound that would pierce through the forest and bring Taylor to her on a cloud or in a gust of wind. But she held in her cry, and it filled her arms and her chest and finally her brain. At that moment, June felt the desire to make something, to create something out of this place, and she decided that she would continue Peter's work. She felt as though there were fire in her blood, and she giggled nervously with the intensity of her feeling. She was blushing, and she walked ahead of Jaru toward the rain shelter, but there was no one there. As they climbed back up the slope, toward the fence, June was full with her self-knowledge: she would make something permanent from this place. Fitzroy might help her, and even if Peter didn't start working again, she would finish the survey herself.

As they walked west, back toward Abini, Jaru began to rush. He pointed to the sky.

"Look," he said, "the rain's coming already."

Dark clouds clogged the horizon, and the day that had been hot and filled with the excruciating glare of the sun was cold now and overcast. Jaru began half-running, half-skipping, and June tried to keep up, but she slipped on the rocks and logs behind him.

"Should we go slower?" Jaru asked.

"No," she said, but she took his hand as she walked across slick logs that crisscrossed the path out of Malvi.

When they had been walking through the downpour for half an hour, June's clothes were cold and heavy against her body. Her boots were weighted down by water and mud. She tripped and fell into a puddle that was thick with pig excrement. Jaru lifted her up and wiped her face with wild sugar cane leaves, and the plant's sharp edges cut into her face so that she bled onto his hands. He spoke to her, but she couldn't hear him through the rain. He took her bag from her and pantomimed with his hands that he would carry her piggyback.

"No," she shouted, "I can walk."

It was sometime after the cloud cover and the sheets of rain had turned the day as dark as dawn and June could not see the path past her feet that she lost sight of Jaru. She looked up and realized that the way was unfamiliar and overgrown—she must have taken a wrong turn in the dark and her confusion. She began to panic. "Oh, god!" she screamed into the rain. She stamped her foot on the ground and felt the squish her sock made inside the boot.

She looked behind her and thought about going back, trying to retrace what she had done, but she knew she would only get more lost and go farther from the path. For a moment she hoped that she was still going the right way, only she didn't recognize it because of the dark and the rain. She stood there, letting the rain pound on her for a few minutes, waiting for Jaru to appear. He would find her. She waved her arms in the dark, circling them like a windmill.

She began to wonder about her faith in the people's knowledge of their land. She had thought the landscape and the people were entwined to the point where they were not distinct from each other. But standing alone on an overgrown path in a darkness that she knew would not relent until the next morning, she became terrified that Jaru did not have complete control over his own whereabouts.

She moved forward, and the farther she went, the more overgrown the path got. Wild sugar cane leaves clung to her as she passed, and her boots got stuck in the muddy earth, pulling her steps slow and awkward. Soon she realized that she was walking in the midst of the bush—there was no longer a path. She was crying in frustration as she continued, and she stumbled and felt how cold and numb she was.

The thought became clear, as though she could read it, that Jaru would not find her. Hopelessly, she kept walking as it got darker and the rain finally eased up. She found a dry patch of earth under a cluster of trees and sat down, and the ground was soft with dead leaves and moss. She knew that she could go no farther in the dark without a light or any idea of a direction. She leaned against the tree and felt how hungry she was. She closed her eyes and spent the night sleeping in brief moments, waking up in terror when a marsupial rat ran across her legs or a bird shrieked in the trees above her.

At dawn June started walking through the heavy brush and finally found a path that wandered through a light regrowth forest. After she had been walking for what seemed like hours, she saw two Abini women emerge at the head of a clearing. As soon as they caught sight of June, they began shouting *"aiyee"* and wringing their hands. The women wore bark-string skirts that were woven thick with *kapul* fur and chicken feathers.

They looked beautiful to June as they ran down the path toward her, holding their swinging breasts to their chests, clucking their tongues, and smiling. They brushed off the dirt and twigs that stuck to June's skin and hair with their fingers, and the younger of the two hugged June, encircling her waist, crushing her damp clothes to her skin. June began to weep while the woman held her.

The two women soothed her, smoothing her hair and talking gently to her in Abini, whispering and murmuring endearments in her ear. They walked her back to the compound, holding her hand and talking the whole way. It was only when she walked up the stairs of her house that they dropped her hands and stood back, shyly smiling at her while she opened the door and went inside to her husband and daughter.

ELEVEN

June liked the house in Abini most in the middle of the day. After breakfast, if it was not raining, she pushed the cut-out window open, and the kitchen filled with mountain air that was warm and clear from the tropical sun. And before lunch, she and Taylor went to their kitchen garden, carrying dented aluminum pots that June had bought in Goroka. They filled them with misshapen plum tomatoes, sweet peas, carrots, cabbages, and fat ears of corn.

During those weeks when Peter was recuperating, June cooked pasta and tossed it with vegetables for her and Taylor. She poured herself a tin mug full of Australian rosé and set the table for the two of them. She and Taylor usually ate in silence, as June watched the day settle around Mt. Philip and drank her wine. It occurred to her that when everything was quiet, and she was alone with her daughter, eating, she felt good and even happy to be in Abini.

She watched Taylor then, in those afternoons, and she felt as if she were seeing her daughter for the first time since she got to the field. The girl was growing—her face looked different than it had in Boston, and her arms and legs were bigger and thicker. Even her clothes had lost their familiar intimacy now that they were ripped, stained, and threadbare. Her face was full of freckles, which made her eyes seem impossibly big and blue, and the hair that surrounded her face was white blond from the sun.

When she was done eating, Taylor pushed her bowl back and announced she was leaving for the gardens or to play with a friend in the Abini river. June marveled at the girl's energy: all she wanted to do after lunch was to crawl into bed and sleep, hiding from the blazing noonday sun. She and Peter had given up trying to force Taylor to do the correspondence course. The girl was too willful, and besides, Peter had reasoned, she had her whole life to learn the intricacies of English—she had only a couple more months here. June listened to Taylor as she went outside, talking with Pende, laughing, and the sound of stones clicking together while they played jacks, and then their faraway chatter and the girl was gone until late afternoon.

June washed the dishes and gave Peter his lunch, sitting with him until he finished his rice and fell back asleep. She sat at the kitchen table, reading Flannery O'Connor, sipping milky, cold tea, waiting for the afternoon rains that brought her daughter back to her.

And then, one day, after breakfast, June decided to go with Taylor to Nari's garden. She followed Nari, Pende, and Taylor as they walked out of the compound, along the Abini river and then up the back of Mt. Biri to the garden. Before the sun became too hot Nari worked, digging with her walking stick into sweet potato mounds, loosening the earth so that she could reach in and drag the tubers out. Her low breasts swayed as she worked, and she sang to the sweet potatoes. June sat under a tree and watched Nari and the two girls playing down the slope from her. What else does my daughter do up here? she thought and watched as the two girls ran into the rain shelter.

"Taylor," June called out, "come here and tell me what Nari is singing."

Taylor poked her head out from the rain shelter and looked up at her mother and back at Pende. For a moment, June thought that the girl would ignore her, but, eventually, she shrugged her shoulders and tramped toward her through the sweet potato ivy. When Taylor got up close to her, June saw that she was flushed and her canvas hat was dark with sweat.

"She's welcoming the sweet potatoes into the sunny day," Taylor said.

June felt embarrassed. Her daughter was annoyed with her and showing it without any hesitation. What had she done wrong? Was it the interruption? Or was it just her presence there, in the garden? June began to blush under her daughter's gaze.

"Don't talk to me like that," she said.

Taylor's expression did not change. She looked at her mother and then down at her feet. She turned around and ran away, her legs brushing through the dense ground cover of ivy. June called to her again, but Taylor pretended not to hear. The garden seemed enormous then, its green hills like waves in an ocean, stretching into forever. June wanted to leave, but she did not know the way home. Nari would insist on coming, anyway, and she would have disturbed the food gathering, and then Taylor and Peter would disapprove.

She watched Nari dig and the two girls pick at weeds and argue lazily. By noon Nari had three piles of sweet potatoes. She leaned against her digging stick and smiled up at June. The sweat on her face and neck and breasts shined in the sunlight.

She pointed to the first pile of sweet potatoes that were thick and purple skinned. *"Thuni,"* she said. She bent down and picked up one from the second pile, *"Mathane,"* she said and showed June how the tuber's brown skin covered orange meat. *"Lathe,"* she said and tossed a tuber with a narrow neck, brown skin, and a milky white inside to her.

Nari walked over to a grove of sugar cane and cut a tall, maroon stalk with her machete. The two girls ran up the hill while Nari cut the cane into four pieces, and then they sat together, in the shade, sucking and chewing the sweet, fibrous bark. Nari began speaking in Abini, pouring long breaths full of words out into the day. The two girls did not respond to her but sat listening, looking out at the garden; Nari would stop talking, draw in her breath, and suck the spit back that had gathered in her mouth.

June wanted to ask Taylor what Nari was saying, but she was still hurt from her earlier rebuff, so she sat there, smiling and uncomfortable. Finally, when Nari paused for a while, June said to her daughter: "You know, Taylor, I'm here to spend time with you."

Taylor looked at her mother. The girl was so remote, like a different person, and June wanted to reach out and shake her. Taylor frowned and turned away, leaning back in the ivy, staring at the Lido mountains. She reminded June of Peter right then with her quiet concentration and the weird half-smile that played on her mouth.

Nari gathered the sucked-dry sugar cane peelings and folded them into a dried pandanas leaf. She made a fire and singed the wet bark, to keep them safe, she explained to June in Pisin, from poison men. During the day, she said, poison men sneaked through the forest, hovering outside of gardens, right beyond the pig fence, watching women dig in the earth. But at night—she shook her head —they crawled over the fence and along the ground, sucking sweet potatoes out of the mounds, searching for anything the women had left behind. They could work poison with bits of hair, sugar cane peelings, excrement, drops of menstrual blood splattered on a leaf, even fiber from a bark-string skirt caught in the boards of a pig fence when a woman hurried out of a garden, rushing to escape the rain. Nari finished burning the sugar cane peelings and leaned against a baru tree.

June waited for Nari to continue, but the woman closed her eyes. The garden was still, baking in the afternoon sun, with only the slow sound of the cicadas carrying through the air. Taylor and Pende took roasted sweet potatoes out of Nari's net bag and began peeling them. Pende offered one to June, and when she bit into it, she realized how hungry she was, and the thick sweet flesh seemed like the best food she had ever tasted. She thought about asking Nari what had happened to Taylor, about what she did every day with her. Did she run off into the forest? Of course, Nari knew, but the garden was hot then and June was full of sweet potato, and she did not ask.

Nari opened her eyes and told them to put the peeled skins on the smoldering fire and then beckoned to her daughter. Pende leaned her head into her mother's lap, and Nari groomed her, slowly pushing her hair from her scalp while she crushed blood-filled lice between her thumbnails.

Looking at Nari with Pende in her lap overwhelmed June. The vision of them seemed large to her and full of emotion. She was awkward sitting there watching; the cloth of her shirt, the leather of her boots enclosing her sock-clad, sweating feet, everything about herself seemed totally out of place.

But then she glanced over at Taylor and almost gasped in surprise. Her daughter was staring at Pende and Nari with ferocious unhappiness. Taylor's face was flushed, and tears were brimming in her eyes.

"Taylor," she asked, "are you all right?"

The girl did not answer. It seemed that she did not even hear, could not understand the English words that hung in the air. She began to cry, a long, loud bawl. Nari shook her head and spoke to Taylor in Abini. Her tone was angry and impatient, and June watched in amazement as Taylor half-crawled, half-walked over and put her head in Nari's lap, lying down next to Pende. Then Taylor started talking, demanding and petulant, through her tears.

"Lice don't like her hair," Nari said in Pisin, laughing. "They don't like the taste of white skin."

Nari ran her fingers through Taylor's hair, pressing her scalp, searching along her ears, down her neck. She scratched the back of Taylor's head and picked through the strands of her fine hair. Taylor's eyes were closed, and her face was wet with tears, but she seemed to be calming down. June felt sick, and the sweet, hot air of the garden filled her nose and mouth. She watched Nari run her hands through Taylor's hair until it was cool enough to start working again.

When they left the garden, the rain clouds were thick on the horizon. June silently followed Taylor and Pende, who walked behind Nari. Nari was bent under an enormous net bag full of tubers, greens, firewood, and bananas. The sun-warmed path smelled strong from pig excrement and mud. She watched her daughter walking, her boots splashing the puddles, and getting mud streaks on her pink skin.

That night, when June gave Taylor her bath, the two of them were uncomfortable with each other. June sat back and let her daughter scrub herself with the washcloth, rubbing her arms and legs until they were pink. June only touched her when she massaged the shampoo into her scalp. She poured a bucket full of hot water over Taylor, rinsing the soap from her skin and hair. She felt sad and hurt. The girl had rejected her so carelessly. She wanted Taylor to apologize, but she realized that the girl did not even know what she had done.

After Taylor went to sleep, June brought the Coleman into the bedroom. Peter woke up slowly, blinking his eyes and staring at her.

"What?" he said.

"You've done this," June said.

"What?"

"I can't even talk about it. It's too stupid to even talk about." June could see the exhaustion in his face, the jaundice in his eyeballs. She imagined how she must seem to him, crazy and angry.

"June, what is it? Why can't you tell me?"

"I just can't. This whole thing is bad, and I don't feel like talking to you."

"But of course you do, or you wouldn't have marched in here with that light blazing and glared me out of R.E.M.- stage sleep."

There it was. She was absurd—marching, glaring. She could not stand herself, and it was too much to be in the room with him.

"Why can't you say anything to me? What are you upset about? Just say it, June. Say it to me."

June stood there, silent, thinking of what she could say to him. Not a word came into her mind. She could not even remember the names of the objects in front of her. She shook her head slowly and walked out of the bedroom with the lamp in her hand, casting shadows and light onto the woven-bamboo floor and walls.

She sat at the kitchen table for a while, listening to the stream that flowed under the house. She pushed out the window and wide moths, their wings mottled black and brown and gray, started flying into the house on the still air, attracted to the Coleman's yellow glow. More and more of the insects flew in until it seemed to June that there were hundreds of the fluttering, huge, tropical creatures surrounding the lamp, slamming into the glass covering, hovering until they fell dead onto the kitchen table. The moths did not stop flying into the kitchen until dawn.

part three

A long time ago, an Abini woman married a man from Nilasa. They killed twenty pigs for the wedding. The girl and her mother, still dressed in their wedding finery, left after the wedding celebrations, crying, with the new husband. The mother and daughter did not want to leave their family, their hamlet, and their beautiful garden. They thought Nilasa was a low place, full of sickness, and it is.

But they went to Nilasa and lived in the man's hamlet. The wife had a baby boy very soon. The husband's family cut a garden for the woman and her mother, but it was small and far away for a woman carrying a baby. It was a hard life for her old mother, whose legs were weak. The ground in Nilasa is dry, and it grows only small and bitter sweet potatoes. The two women had to work very hard for food. And then the husband started to leave them to go hunting. He went for days up in the forest, setting kapul traps. But when he came home, he only ever brought his wife and her mother the animals' skins, no meat. He said that the kapul had been eaten from the inside by a rat. The woman was not happy because she loved to eat kapul meat, but she made hats from the fur and wove some of it into string for her and her mother's skirts and bags.

But the wife's mother got angry. She told her daughter that the son-in-law was eating the meat when he went hunting. The mother told the daughter that she was hungry for kapul meat; she was getting old and felt sick from the poison the Nilasa women had been working on her.

So the next time the husband went hunting, the wife followed him into the rain forest. She watched him set traps and then build shelter for the night. The woman slept under a tree, tucked into a ball, so that no opossums, or birds, or snakes would see her and call out to her husband to warn him. In the morning the wife saw that her husband's traps had caught three big, fat kapul, and she thought, Ah, now my mother will be happy. We will mumu the meat tonight.

But then she watched her husband go to the first trap. He took the eyeballs out of his head and put them on a wide tari leaf. Then he crawled up the tree and into the kapul through its anus and ate all its meat.

When he got back down the tree, he called, "Eyes, eyes, come back to me," and his eyes flew back into his head. Then he took the empty skin from the trap and strung a vine through it and went to the next trap. His wife watched him do the same thing there, and then, when he went to the third trap and crawled into the kapul, she rushed to the leaf and grabbed his eyeballs. When the husband got back down the tree, he called to his eyes, but they could not come to him. The man began to feel around for his eyes, stumbling, walking with his hands out, trying to find his way from memory.

The wife gathered the three kapul skins and her husband's knife from his rain shelter and followed him. He fell down as he walked and got earth and twigs and stones in his eye sockets. He cried out, "Eyes, eyes, come back to me," twice more as he walked, but they did not come—

they were safe in his wife's palm. When they got back to the hamlet, the woman greeted him as though she had been there the whole time. She held her husband's head in her hands and cleaned out his eye sockets—scooping out the dirt and twigs and little stones. Then she licked his eyes with her tongue, cleaning them, and finally she put his eyes back in his head.

"Husband," she said, "you must go to the forest tomorrow and hunt for kapul. My mother is hungry for the meat; she is dying from this bitter earth."

TWELVE

When Peter recovered from the hepatitis he got in Nilasa, he was so thin that his clothes hung loose on his body. He looked in the square mirror over the sink and was surprised at his face—the jaundice was still in his skin, making him seem sallow and dried up; he looked only vaguely like himself. He spoke with Fitzroy over the radio, and they joked about going out for a drink, and then Fitzroy asked him what his plans for the blood survey were. If Peter wanted to get started, he could send out one of the Institute's engineers on an SDA plane to take a look at the generator. The question was easy to deflect through the static, the distance, the endless mountains between them.

I'll let you know, Peter told Fitzroy, when I'm ready to go.

"But why shouldn't he send the guy out now, so the generator can be fixed by the time you're ready to start the survey?" June asked Peter when he walked into the kitchen.

"June, look," Peter said, "can we not discuss this right now?"

He pushed open the window over the table and then walked across the room and opened the window over the sink. A light, moist breeze blew through the kitchen. Peter sat down and began to sip his tea. June stood watching him, her hands on her hips.

"When are you going to start?"

"I don't know. When I'm better."

"You are better."

June walked over to the table and sat down opposite Peter. She draped the red dish towel across the back of her chair and smiled at him.

"What exactly are we doing here if you aren't intending on doing fieldwork?"

"I am intending on doing it. Just not yet."

"I see," she said.

Peter picked up the mug of tea and held it in his hands. June looked out the window and then around the kitchen.

"None of this—not the field work, not the house—none of it is real because I pay for everything. You have no pressure, and you value nothing."

"Look, what are you saying? Why are you bullying me?"

"I'm not bullying you. Now the fieldwork isn't even worth continuing because you don't think it's real."

"Wasn't it you who was here, taking care of me? Have you noticed how sick I've been? Give me a break."

"Okay, then you give me a break. When are you going to start? I'll help you. I'll do anything—I'll go out and gather more information. I'll take Taylor—she can translate. I'll organize the data—I'll type it up. I want to help, Peter. Please."

Peter glanced down at his hands. His knuckle bones protruded through thin skin. He looked up at his wife. Her unwashed dark hair was back in a ponytail and pulled tight so it exaggerated her close-set eyes and her high cheekbones. She is so familiar, he thought. When did I ever not know her face? He was angry then. He curled his fingers up and saw how quickly his hands were white and bloodless.

"I don't know, June," he said. "I'm not ready yet."

"Most people have time limits because their grant money runs out. We have a time limit, too, in case you were wondering."

"Is that a threat?" Peter looked out the window. The idea that she would leave, that he could send her and Taylor back to Boston, occurred to him. He could try to get some money from the British Institute or his department at the university—or maybe even his parents. But then, he knew she wouldn't go.

"Peter, why is everything ruined now?" June asked, and then she began to cry.

"Please, stop, June. Stop."

June kept crying, and her sobs got bigger and filled her chest. She put her hands up to her face.

"I just wanted to make something good for us. I gave you the money my father gave me when he died. It's not nothing, Peter. It's not something to throw away like it's garbage." June was drawing big breaths, and when she took her hands off her face, he saw that it was red and mucus was running from her nose.

"You're getting hysterical," Peter said. He stood up from the table. "I'm not talking about this with you right now."

Taylor came into the kitchen and looked from her mother to her father.

"Please, Peter, please don't leave now, don't leave," June cried and slid off her chair onto the floor. She was bawling then, rocking back and forth. Peter had never seen her get so upset. I don't want this, he thought. Not any of it.

"Go back outside, Taylor," he said.

June began howling, and she reached forward and wrapped her arms around the table leg. Peter watched his wife on the floor, keening, holding on to the table leg, crying and moaning his name. He was annoyed that she was doing this in front of Taylor. He knew that her crying and shouting was carrying through the still day across the compound to Beriapi. It was as if June had disappeared and sent him a lonesome, demanding child. He was so tired. He looked at her and saw himself in another place, in Boston, feeling how he would take care of her and how that made her money his. Have I always pitied her, he wondered.

He saw a eucalyptus tree's silver leaves shimmering in the mid-morning sun out the window. As he stood there, his hands at his sides, she got more worked up. She lay down with her arms and legs stretched out across the floor spread-eagled. Peter bent down and held her in his arms. He could see himself, with June lying on his lap, gasping for air. And he saw how he held his head above her, turned toward the window, so that the smell of her, the heat of her, did not reach his mouth. He knew that she sensed all of him, his guilt, his disgust with himself. He wanted to apologize to her, but he could not.

"Ah, June," he said, "what have we done?"

...

Peter fell asleep after lunch. June went into the office and pulled out the tapes, notebooks, stacked and labeled photographs, and the huge graph paper that Peter had covered with kinship charts. There were eight charts for the seven hamlets of Abini and one that traced the bloodlines of the whole village. She went through his typed-up notes, running her fingers along the printed letters. She opened the Olivetti's red case and wiped the dust off the keys with the corner of her shirt. When she ran a piece of paper through it, she listened to the gears click and roll.

Dear Mother, she typed. We are fine. She pulled out the notebook in which Peter had written an Abini mini-dictionary. There, in his neat black-inked handwriting were the words for mother, father, child, sister, brother, cousin, tall, sick, fat, young, old.

She called Taylor inside and asked her to pronounce the words. Taylor stared at her mother, silent, with large eyes that seemed full of fear. For a moment June thought that she would say something, or refuse to be with her, but she stayed there, quiet, unhappy, and finally began to speak Abini so quickly the words sounded like hiccups in her mouth. June mimicked her daughter and heard how awkwardly her own voice wrapped around the language—she knew she sounded wrong and comical.

"I can't get it right," she said.

"Try, Mom. Try harder," Taylor said.

June looked at her daughter. She was triumphant that the girl was being nice to her, and she felt her chest tighten, and she smiled a slow, bashful smile at her. Taylor nodded her head faintly, as if she were gently agreeing with her mother, as though she understood June's unspoken thoughts. She sat there quietly, patiently repeating Abini words with her mother until the afternoon turned into dusk and June got up to make dinner.

Later that night, when Taylor was already asleep, Peter said that he was going on a trip into the rain forest the following week. He said it would only be for a few days; he said that he wouldn't go if he still felt weak. He said they certainly didn't want a relapse.

No, June said, they didn't want that. He watched her boil a pot of water on the wood stove. She dropped a tin of apricot cake into it, and in a few minutes lifted it out with a wood spoon. She undid the lid with its key, carefully peeling the thin metal into a coiled circle. The cake steamed on a plastic plate, and June cut it into thick slices.

They sat at the table reading in the Coleman's hissing light. When they got up to go to bed, June dropped the cake into the ten-gallon oil drum they used as their garbage can. She banged the lid into place, making sure it was secure against the marsupial rats that crawled through the kitchen during the night.

. . .

Peter walked behind Makino and watched the man's feet slap the ground. Makino's toes were broken and splayed outward, and the skin on his heels was thick and cracked and full of the forest floor's orange earth. He had a small net bag slung over his shoulder, filled with cooked sweet potato, and he carried a wide bow and six arrows in his hand. Makino and the two men behind Peter talked while they hiked up into the forest. They joked and laughed, occasionally switching into Pisin for Peter's benefit, and then back into Abini when they heard a bird call or a rustle in the trees above them.

They stopped at noon and ate. A small stream poured out of a rock face behind them. Makino cut a leaf from a wide vine and formed it into a cup and filled it with cool water for Peter. When Peter held the leaf up to his face, it smelled of black pepper and ginger and rain. He drank three leaf cups full of water. He put the leaf in his canvas bag and rubbed his wet fingers through his hair. Makino and the other men rolled cigarettes and began to smoke and talk.

"*Ai,*" Tilu cried. They all stopped talking and listened.

"*Wannim?*" Peter whispered to Makino.

"It's two moku birds fighting. Two men fighting for a woman, listen."

Peter strained. At first he only heard the collage of bird and insect calls, the loud, throbbing noise that filled the rain forest. But then, gradually, he heard two birdcalls that were distinct, a shrieking h'ya h'ya and then wakaw wakaw.

"Mi harim," Peter whispered. He was excited and smiled at Makino. He wanted to praise Makino's hearing, to say something that would provoke a smile or a confidence. Instead, he became shy and leaned back on his heels and looked up into the trees as though he were searching for the birds of paradise.

The men stubbed out their cigarettes and walked off the path into a thicket of overgrown vines in the direction of the moku birds. The four of them crouched down behind two trees that stood thirty feet tall, covered with moss and hanging vines. Makino pointed up to the branches and Peter saw several birds with huge orange plumes sitting in them and then hopping, jumping around nervously. Peter recognized them. They were raggiana birds of paradise, the bird on the Papua New Guinea flag.

"They're all men," Makino said, "waiting for a woman. They're fighting over the branches—who can stay and dance and who has to go."

And then, as Makino finished talking, a moku flew over them, its enormous tail feathers fanned out and flowing behind, its head covered in iridescent green. It shrieked—ka-caw ka-caw.

"He wants us out, too," Makino said and gestured to the two men behind Peter.

The four of them left, walking quickly, hunched over, stepping gently on the leaves and twigs of the forest floor. After they had walked for fifteen minutes, they stopped at a clearing.

The three Abini men began to cut down wild ginger plants and tear wide leafy branches from trees. They set up a small hut and scattered cut ferns as a carpet on its earth floor. Makino gathered wood and some flat rocks and set up a fire circle right outside the shelter. He lit a fire, and they began to smoke. Peter sat on a wet log and watched the men for a while. They were silent, and he realized that his observation of them was making them uncomfortable. He turned his back and took out his notebook and began to sketch the raggiana that had flown over them, and then he drew the forest floor with its network of vines and roots and rocks that ran underneath it, making the ground bubble.

Makino and the two others were repairing their arrows and turning them slowly above the fire to harden the gummy resin at their joints. The arrows were built from long stalks of wild sugar cane with four prongs of carved, jagged bamboo at the tip. Makino had explained to Peter before they left Abini that the four-pronged arrows were for killing birds—the wide area of sharp, split bamboo was more effective at spearing a small, flying creature. They had also brought other arrows, one with a single thick and narrow bamboo tip that was as sharp as an Okapi knife and weighted at the bottom for killing wild boars and poison men. But as they sat there, at the fire, the men just worked on their birding arrows, tying bark string around the top, melting resin at the joints, and sharpening the prongs with their machetes.

Before it was fully night they went into the rain shelter. Peter spread out his sleeping bag along the ginger-leaf wall and lay down beside Makino. The rain forest was loud. As darkness came, the nocturnal animals woke up and began calling to each other, and the sound overwhelmed Peter. He began thinking about how far he was from his world. If he broke his leg or relapsed into hepatitis, he would die. He thought about the Australians in Goroka laughing at Michael Rockefeller, who, they said, was a pig-headed, rich Yank. Don't want to wind up like ol' Oysters Rockefeller, the *kiaps* said when they didn't want to go on patrol into a dangerous region. Peter could hear Makino's breathing and smell the sweat-and-smoke smell of his skin. He coughed into his hand and shifted his body.

Peter reached under the sleeping bag and touched his journal, his pen case, his Nikon, and his canteen. He relaxed and his eyelids were heavy, and he could feel that he was still sick in his bones and the tenderness of his liver. He thought of June, surrounding herself with effects from home, making a cocoon in their house out of old issues of *Time* magazine, tins of Twinings teas, espadrilles, and sundresses. He smiled then and fell asleep.

...

Peter woke up to the sound of a fire burning wet wood and the pressure of Makino's hand on his shoulder. It was dawn and the forest was vibrating with gray owls hooting and smaller birds hysterically chirping and tweeting, announcing the morning's arrival.

"*Masta,*" Makino said, "*yumi mas harriap.*"

Makino filled Peter's aluminum pot with water and strung it over the fire. When it boiled, he stirred in the mixture of Nescafé, powdered milk, and sugar that Peter had brought from the compound in a plastic bag. He poured the coffee into a yellow tin cup and waited while Peter drank it. As soon as Peter finished, he poured himself a cup and then gave the two other men the rest of the coffee. They ate cold sweet potato and taro for breakfast and set out in the blue dawn for the moku birds' tree.

The tree's branches were packed with birds. Their orange tail feathers and brown bodies clogged the opening in the rain forest canopy, giving the dawn light a dark orange and brown color. It seemed to Peter like there were hundreds of birds there, chattering and squawking, flying back and forth.

"Soon they'll sing," Makino said. "Now they're fighting."

The birds continued to shout and hop around the branches, but then, when a small brown female arrived, they began to bob up and down, and organized their calls into a rhythmic chant.

On a branch at the top of the tree a huge moku spread out his orange tail feathers. His belly was pure brown, and his green face looked side to side. As he shook his body and called out, the other birds became silent. The branch swayed under his movements, and the brown female leaped closer, watching him. Makino pointed to another female who had arrived. The two drab, brown, female birds reminded Peter of Boston pigeons. They were round and so brown he could barely make out their markings. They watched the tree-top as the male swayed, shook, and let out an eerie series of calls that filled the forest with an intense, encompassing hum that sounded like it came from a synthesizer.

And then, while Peter was watching the raggiana display, Tilu shot an arrow up to the top branch and caught the male in the midst of his performance. The bird let out a shriek of rage and then fell with the arrow stuck in his body, bouncing off the branches to the ground. The bird was still alive when they got to it, and it bit Tilu's finger as he picked it up.

"Aiee," he cried out, and the other men laughed at him as he held his bleeding finger. When the bird finally died, Makino pulled the arrow out of its belly and handed it to Peter. He could not believe how small the body was—its plumage had made it look enormous in the treetop. He felt the bird's warmth and stared at its blue beak and the short shiny green and yellow feathers on its head. Its dark blood dripped onto his palms, and he said out loud in English, "You're so beautiful."

Tilu took the bird from Peter. He slit it open from under its beak straight down its belly with his Okapi knife. Then he cracked open its ribs and pulled out its heart and liver and intestines and wrapped them in a wide taro leaf. When he had cleaned out the inside, he strung its orange claws together with a length of cut vine and hung it upside down from a tree branch.

Peter sat on a rock and drew the disemboweled bird in his notebook. The three men said good-bye to him and went back to the moku's tree to hunt for more. He sketched the raggiana's tail feathers, its open beak, and the slit across its body. It seemed to him that after the men left him, in the silence, the bird was still

alive, its flesh not yet aware of its new emptiness. The forest surrounded him with bird calls and the sound of the wind brushing
through the trees. The raggiana's body was swaying, its iridescent
feathers shimmering in the diffuse light.

He willed his mind to be quiet—he lost June, Taylor, Boston, even himself—and he let the dead bird of paradise and the wet
earth smell occupy him as he drew in his book. His pen nib flowing ink onto the page mesmerized him, and he stopped sketching
the bird and began to draw lines and patterns to fill up the paper
with black.

He cracked open the roasted bamboo tube that Makino had
left with him. Steamed greens were entwined around bits of taro
and wild mushrooms. He was hungry, and the food tasted nutty
and full of burnt bamboo. The greens were gritty and oily in his
mouth, and he wondered if they were cooked with pig fat and
thought for a moment of the worms that were filling his blood. He
put the empty bamboo tube down and knew that he was content
to do nothing, to be nothing. He was a speck, indistinguishable from
the water drops that fell from the leaves when the wind blew the
trees. The knowledge that the rain would come and that trees like
the one he was sitting under covered the endless mountains like a
thick spider web filled him. He wondered then if he would remember this feeling or if it would slip away from him and become indistinguishable in the layers of his memory. He closed his notebook.
He could hear the moku calling in the distance.

...

When the men came to find Peter, they had four more male
raggianas with them but none as awesome as the first one Tilu had
shot. They walked through the darkening forest to the rain shelter,
and Makino boiled a pot of rice. He opened two tins of jack mackerel and stirred them into the rice with a stick. He reached into the
pot and scooped handfuls of the rice-and-fish mixture and placed

them in wide tari leafs. He pressed the rice and fish into balls and then handed them out.

The four of them ate and talked in Pisin about shooting the other moku birds. The three men told Peter that the birds had shouted at them when they came back. They hopped down to the lower branches of their tree, ruffled their feathers, and squawked as if they thought they could scare humans the way they scare each other. The birds were as tame as children, they said, easier to kill than a domesticated pig because they didn't know humans.

Tilu and Makino gutted the other birds and filled two bamboo tubes with the meat and put them in the fire. Peter read *The Golden Bowl* while the birds cooked and the three men smoked. He was distracted by the forest, and he could not follow the story, but the English words soothed him, and he read and reread the sentences.

After they ate the rich, tough bird innards, it began to rain, and they sat in the shelter. Makino had lit a fire at the doorway, and it filled the small hut with smoke, and for a while Peter tried to read in the dim light. Eventually, he put the novel in a plastic bag with his notebook and spread out his sleeping bag. The rain continued to fall through the afternoon and into the night. Peter dozed, half aware that the three men were speaking Abini, and later snoring.

Peter woke up from a deep sleep and looked at the luminescent dial of his wristwatch. It was only nine-thirty, but the fire had become deep red embers and the full darkness of equatorial night covered the forest. He listened to the rain for a while and started when he felt Makino's hand lying on top of his sleeping bag. Peter lay there still and listened to the New Guinean man's even breaths, the snorts and coughs from the men, the mucusy sound from their congested lungs. He shifted, and Makino's hand slid down the nylon off the sleeping bag.

The rain was slowing down, and Peter felt wide awake, aware of everything around him: the other men, the light sounds of rain-drops, and the opossums and rats scampering across the ground and nestling into the shelter's leaf walls. Peter began masturbating, slowly at first, his mind full of the rain forest and the sensation of his hand on his penis. He could feel the warmth in his groin, the muscles twinging in his anus, and the closeness of the other men.

He came quickly and wiped the warm fluid onto the ferns next to his sleeping bag. He felt drowsiness crawl through his legs and groin and up his chest to his arms and neck. He listened to the three men breathing and tried to make his own shallow breaths match theirs. The rain started pouring violently again, as though it were the beginning not the end of the storm. It seemed to Peter that the small rain shelter and the trees surrounding it with their wide roots and vines would be washed down the mountainside by the relentless gush of water from the sky.

It was still raining the next day when they packed up camp and started the walk back to Abini.

THIRTEEN

In the morning, when he was still half asleep, Peter listened to his wife as she got out of bed, drew water from the spigot into the kettle, and banged the ashes out of the stove and filled it with wood blocks. He heard her brush her teeth at the kitchen sink and the silence as she combed her hair back into a ponytail and gazed in the mirror. Then heavy steps on the woven-bamboo floor melted into the sound of her rubber thongs slapping the stones that lined the path from the back door to the outhouse.

Peter came back to consciousness with the smell of coffee boiling, rich and burnt, and whispers from Taylor's room sticking in the morning air. June did not look at him when she came back to the bedroom to get dressed. With his eyes closed, Peter listened to her sigh heavily as she buttoned up her pants and rubbed mosquito repellent on her face, neck, the backs of her hands, and then her wrists.

And even when she left the house, Peter saw her in his mind, standing at the front door, a blue bandanna tied under her pony-tail, looking out into the heavy morning clouds that cloaked the eucalyptus trees. He saw how she was resolute—she would not lis-ten to his request that she wait or the promises that he would start working again, just not yet. He knew that as she set out, the square of her shoulders was firm and her long, red boots squished the mud determinedly. She patted her thigh as she walked, drumming a half-formed rhythm.

She insisted that Taylor meet her at a faraway hamlet, and the girl did, good-natured for a while. But Peter knew that at noon, when the sun was blinding and June was standing in the midst of a hot, nearly empty hamlet pointing and shouting in her awkward American-accented Pisin, Taylor would slip away. And in the evening, Taylor whispered to Peter that when she was far away, in the cool, green canopy of a regrowth rain forest, she felt terrible that she had deserted her mother. But he understood then that it was too much for the girl to watch June in a frenzy, ordering be-mused village women in the hottest part of the day to leave the shelter of their huts and put their infants and toddlers in the creased aluminum cup of her scale.

And Peter knew, too, that by the time June noticed Taylor's absence, she was overexcited by her surroundings, by the work of weighing babies and marking the numbers down in long columns of a notebook, and did not feel the truth of it. Eating his lunch alone in the house, Peter thought that in her zeal to organize and record she was like a missionary lady. He saw her urge to take a bar of Lux soap, a bucket of hot water, and clean these people—wash the dirt from their skin, clip their fingernails, bandage their oozing tropical ulcers, and stick them in clean, sensible clothes.

Peter understood that his wife felt these days in the hamlets doing his work without him almost as an awakening—she had developed the colonial administrator's urge for order, sanitation, and regulation. She knew now the salvation implicit in the Christian missionary ladies' crisp pastel shirts, their cropped salt-and-pepper hair, and their sun-wrinkled faces that break into wide, infectious smiles when a native child can finally recite the catechism in English. Peter thought that their cheerfulness, brisk manner, and efficiency were side effects of a euphoria induced from an accomplishment that these white women could never have fathomed in America.

When Peter saw missionary women in Goroka and Port Moresby, he knew that they had found the joy they suspected awaited them in New Guinea, the joy that other women found in love affairs or fabulous, dream jobs. Peter was revolted by their smug authority over the mission's converts, their unself-conscious glee in having so much power over people who could not imagine the striations of the Western, developed world. In their rural parishes their access to cargo, limited as it was, made them glamorous, and they garnered as much excitement and attention as Jackie Onassis strolling down Fifth Avenue. Their intoxication from the place was unmistakable: they filled the post offices and restaurants and colonial administration buildings' offices with their chatter, walking with a well-scrubbed mission *boi,* stopping abruptly when they were confronted with the grim specter of an Australian *kiap* or British medical researcher, their white brethren who looked at them with nauseatingly familiar disinterest.

It was this joy that Peter's wife was beginning to experience on her solitary forays into the scattered hamlets of Abini. He knew it just from her manner and the dry, spare details she used to describe her days.

Peter saw her as she marched home, no longer afraid of the darkening sky and the afternoon downpour that follows on its heels. She arrived at the compound wet, mud splattered, her hands smelling of village children. She made herself a cheese sandwich, a cup of Earl Grey, and filled the canvas shower bag with hot water so that she could wash the day from her skin.

With the Coleman pumped, its cotton bag burning bright, June sat down in the office to carefully type up her work. She filled the house with a rapid clik clak clak, marking a column for girls and then one for boys. She made carbon copies as she went and filed them away among Peter's plastic-bagged papers.

Peter saw all this, knew everything June was doing: he even understood how it was an offering to him—a negotiation, a threat, her resignation. He observed her, as did Taylor, with a mixture of pity and shame. It occurred to him as he lay in bed with his eyes closed, enduring the mornings of her preparations and then the quiet days without her, how far away he had moved from her. He saw her body's movements, the inflections on her face, and the emotions that flickered through her being. It was as though he was observing a friend he had not seen in years from a great distance, curious as to whether she would act like the person he used to know.

FOURTEEN

One morning Nari came to the compound early, while June was still drinking her coffee. She knocked on the wall, and when June pushed open the kitchen window, she said that a woman was giving birth down at the river Abini.

"You can bring your scale," she said in Pisin. "You can weigh the new baby."

June stared at Nari. In the flat morning light the woman's facial tattoos looked so deeply embedded that they seemed part of her skin. June blinked, trying to understand why Nari was there, making this offer to her. She felt shy from the implied intimacy and shocked by the unexpected vision of Nari and her insistence. June wanted to say no, that she could not go with her, but then she thought of the day, of Peter and Taylor's never-ending, wary scrutiny of her. She nodded her head.

"Yes," she said. "I want to come."

The two of them walked to the river, and Nari moved quickly, carrying the scale. They had left Taylor and Pende at the compound because Nari said that the woman giving birth did not want little girls staring at her. Cold from the night before was woven in the morning air, and June breathed it deep into her lungs. Nari was taking her along a path that she had never been on before. It followed a stream that led south from the Abini river, and the banks were heavy with wild sugar cane and tree ferns, which grew dark green and wide. The morning fog clung to the landscape, and June felt as though she were walking into a dream, and then as soon as she thought that, she was annoyed with herself for allowing her mind to wander and become fanciful. She looked up at Mt. Philip in the distance and saw its familiar profile of sub-alpine shrubs encircling the rocky peak, and she felt reassured. How absurd, she thought, that anything in this place makes me secure in my footing.

When they got to the river, the pregnant woman was in labor, squatting in a shallow pooling of water, protected from the ferocious current by a wall of three large boulders. An older woman, her mother-in-law, Nari told June, was holding her around the shoulders, scooping water into her hands, and then dribbling it on the woman's face.

June and Nari watched as the woman gave birth into the flowing Abini, weeping and screaming as the infant's head dropped from between her legs. When the older woman picked the baby boy out of the river, it was red, still covered in mucus and blood, and its eyes were shut tight. Nari took the baby from the older woman and wrapped it in the folds of a stained, green-printed lap lap. She held it out to June. "Here," she said, "you can weigh him."

But June shook her head. She was overwhelmed by the tremendous noise of the Abini and the sight of the baby covered in blood, its tiny body clenched as if in a muscle spasm. The baby's mother was lying back on the river bank, her eyes closed, her legs spread open as her mother-in-law squatted in front of her, helping with the afterbirth.

"I'll do it later," June said.

Nari stood with the baby cradled in her arms and put her lips over its tiny mouth. The infant was screaming, and she laughed at it, and nuzzled her nose in its mouth. How do they live, June wondered, exposed to the world and its merciless germs so quickly? The baby had been born right into freezing cold river water and then surrounded by virulent germs, parasites, and dirt; the germs could kill a fully grown American man. Nari was rocking back and forth, and June wanted to reach her hand out and stay the New Guinean woman. She wanted to say, You musn't kiss it and spread your mouth germs on its face—you mustn't shake it like that. But she did not say anything and watched as Nari gave the infant to its mother and then turned and smiled at her. She picked the scale off the rock and asked, "Later? You want to weigh the boy later?"

June nodded her head and said yes, maybe even another day or in a few weeks. Nari said something to the two women in Abini and then walked away from the rushing river back toward the path, and June followed her. It amazed her that Nari was so casual, acting as though she had been visiting someone's mumu or chatting at a crossroads. The images of the boy's birth were strong in June's mind, and she did not hear Nari at first.

"Wannim?" she asked, distracted.

Nari stopped and turned around to face her.

"Misses," she said. She took June's hand in her own. June was suddenly aware of how much bigger she was than Nari—taller and wider.

"Don't let Mori go out so much," she said in Pisin.

June realized with a shock that this was why Nari had asked her to the Abini that morning. She wanted to talk about Taylor. June began to blush. She looked past Nari at the path and then back at her face. She understood that Nari was about to tell her something awful that she would not be able to recover from, or find her way back to the bright day on the path that led away from the river.

"What is it?" she asked. "What is it that is happening to Mori?"

Nari shook her head and then smiled a small, kind smile.

"I just don't want her to get hurt walking around. She could fall down on a wet log."

June and Nari looked at each other. June knew that Nari was holding back, that she was giving her information with enough room to keep her dignity. For a second, then, as the two women stood on the path, they knew each other's mind. It was perfectly clear between them—Nari's concern, the satisfaction with which she told June about her own child, June's reluctance to hear anything about Taylor, her fear—all of these things were as solid and distinct as the scale in Nari's hand, the mud underneath their feet, and the bruised tanket plants that grew wild along the path's edge. And then, quickly, they backed away, retreating from the intimacy; the confusion of their difference, the language barrier—the impossibility of their connection was between them again like a dark shade pulled over a sun-filled window.

June would be thirty-two next month. She thought about her birthday and wondered how old Nari was. She could be twenty-five or forty-five. June had thought the New Guinean was older than her, but she was no longer certain. Nari's comments about Taylor seemed mean-spirited to her. She didn't like this woman's smugness. Couldn't she see how hard it was for them to be there— so far away from their own, real home? All of a sudden June was exhausted. Her joints ached and her throat hurt, and she wanted to escape from the hot, blinding Abini sun. She wanted to get out of

New Guinea and away from the relentless piling of days that threatened to bury her. What am I doing here? she thought.

"Yes," she said. "You're right about Mori."

...

At dinner that night June was quiet. After she bathed Taylor and put her to bed, she came into the kitchen.

"Peter," she said, "Taylor needs to get out of the field."

"Yes," he said. "I think so, too."

"It's not good for her to be here. It's not good for me, either. I'm sick."

"Are you sick, June? I'm sorry." And then he said, "You're right about Taylor. But what are you saying? Do you want to leave?"

"I don't know. Is that what you want? Do you want me to leave?"

"No, I'm not saying that."

"No, Peter, at least be saying that. At least admit it."

Before Peter could respond, June walked away from him. She went into the bedroom and lay down on her cot. Her joints hurt, and she put her fingers up to her temples. Without taking her clothes off or brushing her teeth or turning down the wick in the oil lantern, she fell into a deep, dreamless sleep.

...

The following day Peter told June that he was going on an expedition with Makino and an older man to collect traditional medicines from the rain forest.

"I'm going to gather what the Abini use when they're sick. You know, bark, moss, roots. I'm going to send them to the lab in Cambridge, have those guys freeze-dry them and study their chemical composition when we get back."

June did not respond. She was sewing a patch onto Taylor's pants, and her throat was sore.

"I think it will be an interesting study. We might find all kinds of things, new antibiotics, narcotics—I'm going to see if there's anyone Fitzroy knows who'd be interested in helping, or maybe funding."

"Peter." June put her sewing down. "That's not what you're here for. You have a half-completed project; you need to finish that first."

June was wearing a blue cotton dress that billowed around her body in the breeze from the window. She was flushed with a slight fever and looked pretty from the heightened color in her face. Peter realized that he had expected her to be enthusiastic; he had wanted her approval.

"I want to do this," he said.

"It's not real science. It's not what you're supposed to be doing."

"Okay," he said. "Please tell me about real science, June. Please tell me what I'm supposed to do."

"I don't care if you don't. But it was a pretty rotten thing to drag me and Taylor into this. At least you could have told me that you weren't serious about anything. You could have said, 'June, we're going to find ourselves in Papua New Guinea. Kinda like the Beatles hanging out with the Maharishi.'"

"I don't have to listen to this."

"I'm sorry," she said, and right then she looked contrite, and he was unsure if she were still angry. "I really am sorry," she repeated.

This time when Peter got ready for his trip, June watched him. She forced herself to notice what he took out of their storeroom: the plastic bags, the mosquito coils, the extra socks, the powdered milk, the matches, the cans of curried duck, the small burlap bag of rice. She thought: I paid for this. I bought this.

"You should write everything down," she said. "Everything you take."

"What?"

"For my taxes. So I can distinguish between your two projects on my taxes."

"Goddamn it, June," Peter said. "What are you trying to prove?"

But in the morning, after he left, June found a piece of graph paper covered with lists of supplies in his neat handwriting.

. . .

In the days after Peter left, June felt sicker and thought that she was getting the flu. She kept working, though, chewing aspirin and drinking water while she weighed babies and took notes. She had told Taylor to come with her on these daily outings, and she was surprised that the girl acquiesced and wondered, fleetingly, if her daughter felt sorry for her. In the mornings, when the two of them left the compound, they walked together talking and reciting A. A. Milne rhymes until they passed Beriapi and Taylor's friends ran out to join them.

On the fourth day that Peter was gone June's sore throat got so bad that she could not swallow. She had walked to a small garden near the hamlet Tavitai to weigh a newborn girl. After she weighed the baby she put a Callard & Bowser butterscotch in her mouth. She sat on the ground under a banana tree and put her palms down on the soft, black, sun-warmed earth. The smell of pigs hovered in the air, and the tree's roots pressed into her buttocks. Taylor squatted down next to her, and her daughter's breath, her skin, made June feel flat in the sickness.

"Taytie," she said. "Let's go home. Mommy doesn't feel good."

Taylor helped her mother to her feet. As they walked to the compound, June kept stopping and leaning against the earth wall that ran alongside the road. June could feel an ache in her spine and a tingly sensation that ran across her hips and down her legs. Jesus, she thought, now I'm sick.

When they climbed over the hill that led down to Beriapi, Tinu came and met them. An old man from Tavitai had called out the news that the white woman was sick. It seemed as though the entire hamlet of Beriapi had gathered at the pig fence on the edge of the road to see what was going on. Tinu walked over to June and picked her up. He carried her piggyback the rest of the way to the compound. The pounding rhythm of his body and the smell of his skin made June nauseated, but she was grateful that she did not have to walk anymore; she could not ever remember being so sick. When Tinu lay June down on her cot, he said that he would send two boys to run to the forest to get Peter.

Taylor unlaced her mother's boots and covered her with a blanket. June began to shiver.

"Mom, what is it?" Taylor asked. "What do you have?"

June could not open her eyes, and her lips were pressed together in a bloodless, light pink line. Taylor began sniffling, and Tinu's voice carried through the room. Was he in the house? June could not tell for sure, but when she thought that Taylor had asked him to come inside, she felt uneasy and nervous that the New Guinean man was in her house, alone with her daughter. Her teeth began chattering, and her bones felt cold inside her hot flesh. June felt the realization that something serious was going on in her body slowly crawl into her conscious mind. And then, as if her fever had slowed down her reactions, she recognized the terror, as distinct as a siren, wailing in her head. Taylor was gone, in the kitchen drawing water from the spigot, and then she heard Peter. It was not him, though, just Tinu; the deep masculine tones had confused her.

She sensed Taylor by her side and wondered how long the girl had been there.

"Taytie," she said, "Mommy needs you to get the medicine box and get me some pills."

The box was in the storage room, and its smooth, white surface and red-painted cross were as clear to June as if she could see it. In another life she had gone to a medical supply shop in Boston and bought bandages, creams, and baskets full of plastic pill bottles and stuffed the bottles with erythromycin, Valium, antimalarials, Lomotil, aspirin, Dramamine, and a dozen sheets of birth control pills. When Peter had found her organizing it, writing neat labels and taping them to the bottles, boxes, and tubes, he said that she was as equipped as an astronaut going to the moon. NASA could not be more thorough to protect against encounters with alien life, he had said, laughing.

June heard Taylor open the box and then the bottles, rattling their tablets as they fell to the floor.

"I need quinine," she said. Her eyes were still closed, and she felt Taylor's small fingers playing in her hair, undoing the bandanna that was wet with sweat. June was alone then, far away, and she forgot where she was.

"I don't know which one that is, Mom," Taylor said.

And June was there again, in the field; her daughter's voice yanked her back into the present.

"It's a white pill," she said. "The label says quinine."

She heard Taylor walking on the floor and then the soft weight of twenty bottles on top of her belly. The bottles slid over the blanket, filling up the gutter between her body and the wall.

"How do you spell quinine?" It was Taylor's voice, but the question seemed impossible, absurd—none of the words made sense, and then it was a riddle, and June tried to stack the words on top of each other.

"Mom, Mom," Taylor shook her, and the pain radiated from her head to her chest.

"I have malaria," she said.

That was the answer to the puzzle, and she was pleased that she had said it. She became hot, sweating, and the two-way radio screamed to life, buzzing, filling the house with its cackle and far-away voices fading in and out.

What was her daughter doing, running away? Taylor was always running, angry, hiding, her body kissed with a rash that crawled up her ankles, encircled her legs, and made her red and raw. She would never talk to June seriously, the girl dodged any-thing real; she only ever stared at her mother with her big eyes, so blue and flat.

"Mr. Fitzroy—Abini," Taylor was singing from the other end of the universe, "over and out."

The cackle and hiss of the radio faded out, and then it was a missionary in Kainantu ordering his supplies from Steamships. June wanted to call Taylor into the room, and tell her what? June was full of her daughter then, and she wanted to calm the girl and wipe the sweat from her face and fill her mouth with water. Taylor was with her, floating, while June reached up and caressed her, wiping the mucus from her nose with one of their Chinese tea towels that were printed with red apples. Daughter, she thought, forgive me.

June could hear Dennis Lowther's South African accent over the radio. Lowther was Fitzroy's assistant, and she was surprised to hear his voice, and she became disoriented. What was Taylor saying? She could not hear the words, only the click-click of the handset.

June was gone, floating in the evening air, hovering over Abini. She was full of a thick sadness that felt like a drug, injected into her blood, washing over her bones and organs, making her weep. She knew she was crying and felt how dry she was—not even enough water for a tear. She was missing someone, wanting again; the familiar lonely ache wrested itself from her mind until it was dancing on the blackened plane with her, taunting, hissing, smiling like a snake.

When she came back to the room, Taylor was kneeling at her side, and June said: "I have to pee, Taytie. Get me a pan."

And then Taylor was pulling back the covers, unbuttoning her mother's pants, and they were both surrounded by the smell of stale urine, for June had already pissed in the bed several times without knowing it, and the strong, unwashed odor from her vagina. Taylor held the bowl under the bed and then helped her mother up, hugging her around the waist. June crouched over and pissed dark yellow urine into the bowl.

"Oh, god," she said. As she leaned back in bed, Taylor covered her with a blanket. June listened to her daughter's footsteps and then the sound of the metal bowl clanging into the sink as Taylor poured her urine down the drain.

June shifted, moaned, and breathed heavily, fading into unconsciousness and the intense heat of her malarial fever. She was shivering, and throughout the night she did not feel the cool cloth on her forehead or her daughter's whispering kisses.

...

In the morning Nari was outside the house and then in June's bedroom shaking her head, clucking her tongue.

"Aiee," she said. "Someone worked big poison."

Nari brought the smell of Beriapi and wood smoke with her, and she squatted on the floor and chanted a low, tuneless song. June began moaning, and Nari went over to the bed, slid her hand under the blanket, and patted her breasts. She began cooing, talking to June in Abini as if she were a baby. June opened her eyes. She licked the lines of dried blood that outlined her lips. She looked from Nari to her daughter. She was confused then and scared.

"Please get her out of here," she said. "Oh, god." She started crying. She watched her daughter motion for Nari to leave the room, and she was angry that the girl seemed to regret the New Guinean woman leaving.

"Get her out, Taytie. I can't stand the smell," June tried to shout, but her voice was just high-pitched and crackly. Nari turned around and stared at June, and the white woman retreated into her sickness, avoiding the anger that the other woman filled the room with. She just wanted her gone.

Taylor spooned Tang into her mother's mouth, and June coughed and spit. She rolled her head to the window. She was pulled out of a hot, uncomfortable sleep when her covers were pulled back.

"Taytie," she asked sleepily, "what is it?"

Taylor ran her hand along her mother's back and then through her tangled, dirty hair. June tried to stretch her legs out so that her daughter would have more room. Taylor stayed in bed with her, her arms wrapped around June's chest, while her heart beat slow and strong and filled the silence between them. June's skin coated Taylor with sweat, and the girl fell asleep like that, and the two of them did not dream.

FIFTEEN

The runner reached Peter's camp at midnight the second day after he left Abini. He was a teenage boy, and he arrived breathless, wearing a pair of threadbare khaki shorts that were split over the muscles of his thighs. The boy was terrified from his trek through the dark; he had worried about poison men since he left Abini. He clutched a bow and two pig arrows in his hand while he told the men how sick June was. He said that she had fallen on the road outside Beriapi shaking with fever. He said that Taylor was alone in the house with her mother, crying, filling the night air with her weeping.

As soon as the runner finished his story, Makino, Litu, and Peter packed up the camp. There was only a kerosene lantern and a small flashlight among the four of them to light the way, and they stumbled over roots and vines in the moonless night. Peter smacked into a wide tari tree, and his left eyebrow swelled up and throbbed while he walked. The prickly fur of hanging vines caught him and burrowed through the cotton of his clothes and stung his skin as he wove on and off the path.

When he got to the house, he pumped the Coleman, and as it hissed with light, he saw the dirty dishes, Cadbury bar wrappers, and tins of food strewn around the kitchen. The supply room door was open, and when Peter went to close it, a lean, furry rat scurried across his boots and into the hole under the sink. He walked into the bedroom holding the lamp in front of him. The light wavered, casting about the room, picking out June lying in bed, her mouth slack-jawed, her eyes shut, and pill bottles scattered on top of her, on the bed and floor, and finally Taylor, curled in a fetal position at her mother's feet.

"Taylor," Peter said, nudging his daughter. "What's going on?" He squatted down and picked up two pill bottles that were on the floor.

"Mom needs quinine," she said. The girl squinted at him as her eyes adjusted to the light.

"Goddamn it," Peter said. "Jesus Christ." He read the labels on the pill bottles in his hand and asked, "Where are the quinine pills?"

Taylor shrugged her shoulders. She looked down at the floor and began to cry. Peter saw himself then, storming into the house, filthy, smelling of sweat and smoke, waking her up after she had been all alone with her sick mother for days. He heard the two-way radio, the crackle and buzz and high-pitched call of hundreds of transistors across the Highlands and down to Moresby and the coast.

"I'm sorry, Tay," he said.

He put the lamp on the floor and began picking up pill bottles until he found the quinine. He unbuttoned June's shirt and saw the rivulets of dried Tang on her neck and breasts and the spit that had gathered in the corners of her mouth.

"June," he whispered.

But she was sweating, full of fever, and her eyes stayed closed. Peter went to the kitchen and mashed the quinine into powder between two spoons. He drizzled honey into the powder and then stirred the mixture with a toothpick until most of the grains dissolved.

He held the back of June's head in his hand and gently put a spoonful of the drug-filled honey between her chapped lips. June coughed and then swallowed the thick liquid. Peter got a washcloth and cleaned her face and neck. Then he picked up Taylor, who was sitting watching him, and carried her into her room. When she was lying on the cot, he kissed her and pulled the blanket over her body.

"Don't worry, Tay," he said. "Everything is all right."

She nodded her head. As Peter stood above her, he saw how little she was. She took up less than half the cot with her legs curled up against her belly. Peter thought that she looked like an angel in the uneven light. Her hair framed her face with loose curls, and her full red lips were frowning, holding back a sob, and freckles crisscrossed her skin. He wished then that she was still only his and that he had never brought her so far away from her room in Boston.

He bent down and kissed the girl's cheek, feeling her smooth skin under his lips. He put his fingers in her hair and said, "I won't leave you again, Taylor." He watched his daughter shut her eyes and ease into unconsciousness. He wondered what it was that she might want to hear from him.

At four A.M. Peter opened the window over his cot. He took off his hiking boots and peeled the wet, wool socks off his feet. Several sleepy, blood-fat leeches spilled onto the floor from his socks.

He picked them up gently and laid them across the palm of his hand and took them to the kitchen garbage.

When he came back to the bedroom and began unbuttoning his shirt, he saw that June's eyes were wide open. Peter started, unnerved that she had been watching.

"June?" he asked. He went to the kitchen and got her a mug of water and held it to her mouth. She watched him while she sipped the water. Peter took a glass jar of Vaseline from the medicine box and rubbed the jelly onto her chapped lips.

"Are you all right?" he asked.

She looked at him. Her eyes seemed clear and clean of fever.

"Peter, why didn't we record birth weights?"

He saw then that he was wrong; she was not herself. She was intent and awake from the fever. She acted as though she had been waiting up all night to ask him this. But he knew that she had just been sleeping; she was delirious.

"The birth weights are very important. We must record them."

"We will, June. We'll record them. Try not to worry."

"Yes, but why didn't we think to do that?"

"I don't know," Peter said. He smiled at her. "I guess it didn't occur to us."

"But you see, don't you, how that would make all the difference in the world."

She's babbling, Peter thought. He wanted to laugh then, to point out to her how silly she was but how herself, how she was totally her, even when she was febrile and hallucinating. He knew she was terrified, and he felt enormously sorry. He wished that he could reach into her soul and show her that he was there.

"June, I'm right here with you. You know that, don't you?"

She stared at him and then blinked and rolled her face to the wall.

"I just don't know why Peter didn't think to do that," she said. Who was she talking to about him?

"We can still do it, June."

"I always said that it was what we needed to do."

June started shaking, and Peter realized that she was crying. For the past few months in the field she had cried so easily, so quickly—over nothing—over a small fight with Taylor or when they could not get a radio connection to the British Medical Institute. She was crying again, then, when she was full of fever and hallucinating, not even knowing what was wrong or why she was upset.

Peter sat on the floor and held her hand. He was exhausted, and he could hear the dawn approaching through the window. He looked at the sweat on her face and neck, the oil in her hair. He was impatient for her fever to break and the night terror to dissipate. She would be so much better in the morning. He mashed up an aspirin for her and wiped a cool cloth over her face. She started shaking again, and Peter sat with her, feeling miserable.

The roosters began calling from their chicken coop, and dawn was filling the air with its blue light.

"June," Peter said. "It's your birthday, baby." He kissed her palm.

"Yes," she said. "That's what we needed to do."

She understood her husband, though, and even knew that her response was wrong—that he would think that she was too sick to understand him. But it was only that she was somewhere else and could not control the words that flew from her mouth. She was there with him, so close that she could sense his worry, his impatience, the pressure of his fingers on her hand, his breathing. She wanted him to continue, to explain everything to her. But she was also stuck behind him, in the moonless Abini night, unable to catch up with the day that was spreading over the mountains.

She was trying to remember something—what had she for-gotten? It nagged at her as she heard her husband from the corner of the enormous room—was it a room? No, she was alone in an empty wild place, a place like the rain forest but with no trees or rocks covering the mountains.

Taylor was in front of her for a second, and then the vision of the girl evaporated as quickly as an image shook from a kaleido-scope, and she was filled with an immense craving for her. She called out to her daughter, but the sound she made was only a moan, and Peter—she could see him so clearly then—did not know what her distorted cry was or where it came from. She wanted her daughter—her skin, her small hands, the feel of her hair, the smell of her breath. A panic began invading her. But she did not feel the anxiety; she simply saw it as clearly as the burning Abini sun rising in the blackest part of a midnight sky.

"Taylor," she said, but the word came out again as a blur of vowels. But as quickly as she said her daughter's name, the girl was gone from her mind. It was as though she lost her, and not even Taylor's afterimage was burned into the hot, impossible place she was suddenly in. She longed for the darkness to come back. The light burned her eyes, and the sounds of the day, which were dis-tant at first, were closer now and excruciating. Her own body, with its blood pumping through her legs and arms and heart, pained her skin.

June opened her eyes, and for a moment she saw Peter sitting at her side. She focused on him and brought herself back from the images and noises in the corners of her mind. Even when she had to shut her eyelids from the pain, she saw him and knew exactly who he was. He filled up her entire being with his familiar face and voice. Was he talking then? She was not sure if he was or what he was saying. She had to open her eyes again; she had to see him and ask him the question that she finally remembered. What had he done this for? Why wouldn't he stop? Stop, she screamed in her mind. She felt her anger become sleek and begin to move like a pebble rolling down the slope of a hill. She closed her eyes and felt the sourness in her mouth. How had she come to be with him? She did not want to die.

She missed her own mother then, and fleetingly wondered where she was. But even in her haze, she was only really thinking about Peter. She realized how the thought of her husband had always been in the forefront of her mind. He was so silent. This was the way he had made her desperate and she had followed him, searching. She had believed that somewhere in the details of an everyday life with him she would find him and he would stop the ache that filled her bones and made her chest tight. But Peter was so elusive, always far away in his work, in his distraction, concealing what she knew was there, wrapped up like a child's present and thrust into the depths of a closet, hidden but acknowledged. She could not think of a time that she had lived without the silent threat that he would leave her, and it kept her dancing, needy, at the door of his being. She felt as though she was always following Peter around Cambridge, to New Guinea, throwing her money at him. Secretly, she had thought that he understood how completely alone she was and that he saw the impenetrable shield of her soul. Just the idea that he might understand this had made her crazed to be with him.

June had been perpetually hungry for her husband from the moment she met him, and she had thought that he had been stingy with his essence, selfish, giving her only a trickle, a drip drop at a time. But as she lay there, her head swirling, feeling the anger in her soul burning as hot as the malaria, she saw that she had been wrong. Peter had concealed nothing from her: he had nothing hidden, there was nothing for her. What she got from him was what he had.

And then she felt his fingers on her hand. Without willing it, the darkness came back. It was the soothing, easy cool of night, and she knew she was slipping, forgetting everything, falling into a hole. She let go, reassuring herself that the hot was gone. Only the sour sickness in her stomach and the knowledge, the conviction, that there was something wrong that she could not see or name, made the sensation of falling an unpleasant one. But soon June felt even her terror as beside the point and was as puzzled by it as the bumps in the landscape that she could no longer escape.

And then, out of the nothingness she heard the flutes playing. The throbbing high-pitched call of the lead flute overlaid the back-and-forth rhythm of the deeper, chorus ones. Her body was filled with the music, and she floated along its melody, sure then that she would remember herself. And in the time it took for the heavy clouds that ring Mt. Philip to release their rain, June knew that she had finally found her husband. Some time after this realization bled into the jumble of her anger, she was gone.

S I X T E E N

The morning he was scheduled to fly to Abini, Mitch Kinsey had stood in the Seventh Day Adventists' shack on the Goroka airstrip and stared gloomily at the mountains that lay east. He worried that heavy clouds in the Abini range would clog the flight path on his way back. He drank a thermos of Nescafé and scratched his head, trying to find an opening in the gray morning sky.

Mitch had always been superstitious, and he refused to fly if things were not "on." If a New Guinean, passing by the airstrip, made an inscrutable comment about the weather or the destination he was headed for, Mitch would rub his palm over his great bald head and take it as an omen as damning as a dark, thundering rainstorm on the horizon.

"The savages aren't for it," he would say in explanation to an exasperated engineer from Texaco or British Petroleum who would stand staring at a perfect blue sky over the airstrip and fume at Mitch about contracts. "Y'can fly with the Holy Rollers," he'd say and jerk his thumb at the Seventh Day Adventists' flight shack.

The threat of the Highlands rains unnerved Mitch. Their violence seemed arbitrary and punitive, filling the sky with a fury that he was sure was pointed at him. Even though he liked flying anthropologists and engineers over the winding brown rivers, mountain forests, and flat grasslands to airstrips that were cut out of the green wild, he always felt his death so close that it was in his mouth when the plane's engine roared to life.

...

By the time Joe Radley, the SDA flight manager, brought a canvas sack full of mail into his shack, he knew he would get to Abini and back with the corpse of the American woman.

"It's 'kay, Mitch. You'll be right," Joe said when he saw Mitch standing there looking to the mountains.

"Yeah," he said doubtfully.

Mitch had not flown with a dead body since he flew resupply in Vietnam as an RAAF pilot. He knew the feeling that would crawl through his spine to be enclosed in a metal cage thousands of feet above the earth with decaying flesh. Poor woman, he thought. He remembered June and her family. He had seen them in Steamships, at the Goroka pool, eating at the Bird. He had even spoken with Peter Campbell a few times when he had been with Tony Fitzroy. Mitch had thought June was attractive in an odd, nervous way. Not his type, but she had made an impression on him, enough so that he was shocked and upset to hear that she had died out in the bush.

The story of June's death sounded strange to him. He never heard of a white person dying in Papua New Guinea except for the occasional crazy missionary and rich, adventuring American. Maybe it was something else, or the woman had refused to take her antimalarials. Thinking about June's death and the clouds gave Mitch a bad feeling. He looked at the mailbag. He was stopping at a Christ Church mission in Okapa first. He decided that if the clouds were still heavy when he got to Okapa, he would turn around and leave the American woman in the field for another few days.

...

When Mitch flew through the corridor between Mt. Philip and Mt. Abini, he saw the crowd that had gathered to meet him. The Abini natives had planted poinsettia around the airstrip, and as he circled and brought the Cessna's nose around for the descent, the flowers looked like bloody dashes against the dull green of the day.

He brought the plane down and sat in the cockpit for a few minutes listening to the engine slow. A group of small boys, dressed only in rag loincloths and tanket leaves, were standing huddled together. As soon as the propeller stopped and Mitch opened the door, they came running at him shouting, *"Mornin, masta!"*

The rest of the crowd was quiet and regarded him with subdued expressions. He looked around until he saw Peter Campbell, standing alone. Mitch waved at him and patted the boys' heads.

"Mornin, monkis," he said to the boys.

Mitch stepped out of the plane, and the boys sucked in their breath and then exploded in giggles. His tall frame and bald head that shone as bright as the plane's aluminum siding in the sunlight delighted them. The boys reached out and gently touched his pants and the back of his shirt as he walked past them toward Peter. Mitch did not mind the New Guineans as he had the Vietnamese. Their reddish skin and the distinctive sour smell of their bodies seemed a part of the rolling valleys that became sharp-edged mountains as he flew east out of Goroka. He liked the people in Abini, and he reached out and took a little boy's small, dirty, brown hand in his enormous pink one, exciting the child so much that he burst into tears.

Peter looked bad. He hadn't shaved for days, and he had dirt smudges on his face. His clothes were soiled as well, and he seemed dazed. Mitch had rarely seen a white man look so far gone in New Guinea. He agreed with the unspoken rule that whites in-country should be especially careful of their appearance; it was an important distinction—those who were dressed and those who were naked.

As Mitch looked at Peter, he thought, Americans are different; they're looser, less dignified. It seemed to him that somehow even the slow drawl of their accent pointed to a casual disregard for the place that led to poor June Campbell's death. Still, Peter was pathetic, and Mitch felt sorry for him.

"You holdin' up, mate?" he asked.

"Oh, yes," Peter said. "We're fine."

Mitch had forgotten about the Campbells' little girl, and he looked around for her. Peter pointed at the group of children surrounding the Cessna. A little white girl was standing back from the crowd, watching while they poked and prodded the plane's undercarriage.

"Crikey, she's really one of the savages, isn't she?"

As soon as the words were out of his mouth, Mitch regretted them. He heard his own voice, nasal and clipped, hang in the still Highlands air, leaving a residue between him and the other man. The girl had started walking toward them, looking at the ground. But Peter seemed not to have heard him, and he only nodded his head and smiled into the distance. He looks barmy, Mitch thought. What happened to his wife? They had been playing some kind of game out here. Mitch shook his head without meaning to.

"Ya comin' with me?" he asked.

"No," Peter said. He gestured, pointing to the path that led away from the airstrip. "I've got to close up the house. My daughter—I—"

Mitch nodded, waiting for him to finish. But Peter just stood there, with a slight smile on his face, gazing at the mountains. The clouds were thickening, and Mitch had a sudden terror of being stuck in Abini for the night with a dead body and this American and his daughter.

"I need to be going soon, mate," Mitch said.

Peter nodded then and looked at the crowd gathered around the Cessna.

"Yes," he said, "I can imagine that you would."

Peter seemed agitated by the Abini villagers paying so much attention to the plane. How weird, Mitch thought. He wants me gone. And then the thought floated across Mitch's consciousness that Peter was jealous of him and wrapped up in the villagers' relationship to him as the white man. Mitch knew *kiaps* like that. But the idea quickly submerged into his soul, leaving only a disquieting dislike of Peter in its place. The thought of June Campbell, alive, walking around Goroka with her dark hair and large breasts, became clear in his mind. Shit, Mitch thought. This is all wrong.

"What happened?" he asked. "Can you tell me?"

Peter shook his head. "Malaria," he said. "I was away when she got sick."

"Jesus Christ," Mitch said. "Was she alive when you got back?"

"I don't know," Peter said. Seeing the look on Mitch's face, he said, "I don't remember."

"I'm really sorry, mate," Mitch said.

Peter smiled at him. "Thank you."

Mitch hated that he had agreed to fly out to Abini.

...

Peter and three village men carried the corpse to the plane. Mitch strapped the body, which had been covered with sewed-up sheets, to the back seat.

"Uh, Tony Fitzroy's meeting me and taking care of all this in Goroka?" Mitch asked.

"Yes," Peter said and then fixed his gaze on Mitch.

For the first time since he landed, Mitch felt the other man really notice him. But just as quickly, Peter was gone again, the same emotionless smile spreading across his face.

"Thanks a lot," Peter said and looked into the mountains, shielding his eyes with his hands against the brightness breaking through the clouds.

"No worries, Peter," Mitch said.

He wanted to ask what had really happened out there. He wondered if he should insist that this man come back with him, or at least his daughter. Was there something legal he was supposed to do? It occurred to him that Peter might have killed his wife. Relax, Kinsey, you're getting all worked up, he thought to himself. He looked down at Taylor and saw that there were tear streaks on her dirty face, and he shook his head. The poor kid. He knew he should get her out of there, but then he saw Peter put his hand on the girl's shoulder protectively, as if the other man sensed his thoughts. Jesus, Mitch thought, I'm not a bloody policeman.

As Mitch flew away from Abini with the American woman in the back of his Cessna, he could not calm his mind. He did not understand what had just happened with Peter Campbell, or why he had such a strong feeling that he had made a mistake. It's only death, he thought. I forgot what it was like to be close to it, to see what it does to everyone surrounding it. Death is a violation of a person, especially out here, among the savages. He thought of June's husband on the airstrip in Abini, and he was embarrassed for her.

When he saw the kunai grass and metal roofs of Goroka, he thought, of course, there was nothing that he could have done differently in Abini. He was impatient to land and get away from June Campbell's corpse.

SEVENTEEN

Peter arrived with Taylor and Makino at Tavitai after two o'clock. The sun was extreme, and on the walk up the mountain his face, scalp, and the backs of his hands were burned pink. Makino carried Taylor most of the way, grasping roots and tree trunks when the steep incline threatened to topple him backward. Taylor was wearing Peter's wide-brimmed canvas hat and a torn green dress that dropped down to her knees. Once they were in the hamlet, she stood behind her father, grasping the belt loops on his pants, hiding from the villagers' gaze the way she did when they were first in the field.

    A skinny hunting dog ran out of the black interior of a hut. The dog circled around Peter and Taylor, yapping and barking until Makino kicked it. Peter unzipped his nylon bag, took out his felt-covered canteen, and drank from it. Makino spoke to the people who came out of their huts, explaining to them in a mixture of Pisin and Abini that the white man was going to take some of their blood.

Tavitai was considered a low-status hamlet by the rest of Abini—the place was inconvenient and remote. Only old women, people without extended families, and widows who were considered unlucky and unmarriageable lived there. Makino was brusque when he talked to these people and looked out at the mountains or at Peter so that he seemed distracted and only vaguely aware of their presence. The people in the hamlet looked bemused, and a few children walked toward Peter and Taylor slowly, with wary expressions.

Peter glanced at the assembled villagers, and when Makino gestured to him, nodding his head, he emptied his bag and spread it on the ground, smoothing it down with his palms. He carefully lined up a bottle of rubbing alcohol, cotton-gauze squares, plastic-capped syringes, glass vials, and a black wax pencil. A young woman with a baby propped on her hip came and looked at Taylor and the blood-gathering paraphernalia. An old man with pupils that were light blue from cataracts began shouting at Makino and waving his arms.

"*Masta,*" Makino said after the man had finished, "they want to be paid."

Peter looked around at the crowd that gathered near him. They were standing on the dry, dark earth of Tavitai, hugging their arms to their chests, squinting against the bright light. Taylor was squatting under a tree by herself. It was the first time anyone from Abini had asked Peter directly for money. He looked out at the unadulterated afternoon light flattening the color from the mountains. He waited for Makino to say something about the money, but the man was quiet then, looking intently at the bag spread on the ground.

For some reason that he didn't understand, Peter felt ashamed. He sensed that he was being treated differently than he was used to, and that the old man was being disrespectful of him. He wished that Taylor would come and translate for him. He hated that he didn't understand the rapid *aya a yuma na aya* sound of Abini.

Peter only had seven kina with him, and he took the colorful notes out of his pocket and handed them to Makino. Makino held the bills over his head and made a speech in Abini, gesturing at Peter and then the syringes that lay on the bag. Peter looked over at Taylor, but she was not paying attention. She was playing a halfhearted game of jacks with some pebbles. Finally, the old man came forward and took the seven kina from Makino.

Peter began drawing blood from the young woman with the baby. He wrapped a yellow rubber cord around her arm and wiped the soft hollow of her inner elbow with alcohol. He pressed the needle into her bulging anterior cubital vein, and the glass vial filled with dark red blood. A few old women were standing close to her, watching, and they clucked their tongues and wrung their hands.

"*Ita ita,*" they said in alarm as Peter pulled the thin metal needle from her skin.

Peter continued drawing blood. He got a rhythm going, swabbing, pricking, drawing, and then bandaging the tiny, bleeding circles he made on their skin. Peter wrote labels on the tubes with his wax pencil. Female, he wrote on one of them. Post-menopausal. Finally, he felt the thoughts that whirled around him, making him unsteady, quiet down. He saw how important this work was. Just the idea of the particles, the life, the miculla in the blood he was filling the glass vials with relieved him. He smiled at the people as they lined up in the hot, dry afternoon. They were grim and silent as they thrust their arms at him, and he smiled and even began whistling for a while.

But he was nervous, also, and his balance was delicate, so when Makino asked him a question as he inserted a syringe into a young boy's arm, he got distracted. He jabbed the child, and then in his confusion pushed the needle further and ripped through the top layer of his skin. The boy started screaming as his blood, bright red in the light, dripped down to the earth.

Peter shouted, and his loud voice filled the still hamlet with alarm. The boy ran away with the needle still stuck in his arm. Makino and the boy's mother ran after him and brought him back to stand in front of Peter. The child was naked and skinny, and his distended belly protruded, partially hiding his small penis. He ripped the syringe out of his own arm and threw it over the fence into the sunburnt stand of coffee trees.

Peter bandaged the boy's arm, wrapping white gauze and tape to his brown skin and then smoothing the whole thing with his fingers.

"*Sori,*" he said and smiled.

His mother smacked the boy on the back of his head and frowned at Peter. She stuck her own arm out, indicating that he should take her blood instead. But Peter had already drawn blood from this woman, and he realized that she thought he just wanted more; Makino had not explained that he needed specific blood, not large quantities. He was irritated that none of these people understood what he was doing there.

"I am looking inside the blood," Peter said in Pisin to the woman. He gestured with his fingers, making circles in the air. "I am finding little animals in the blood."

The woman did not respond, and Peter asked Makino to translate for him. Makino started speaking in Abini, shouting at the woman and shaking his fist at the boy. Makino did not understand, either. Peter shook his head no. He was crestfallen then and felt the sweat on his face and the sharp sting from his sunburn.

"Asawa bilon mi," he said. My mistake.

There were fourteen tubes of blood. He placed them in a plastic bag and cushioned them with leftover cotton gauze, making sure they would not smash into each other. The afternoon clouds gathered on the horizon. Makino pointed to them and said they needed to hurry so that they did not get caught in the rain.

The walk down the mountain was steeper and more difficult than Peter remembered. Taylor fell down twice, tripping on the roots that had helped Makino carry her on the way up. Peter looked at his daughter and felt badly for her. She was crying again, the soundless, weirdly calm crying that she had done for days whenever she felt uncomfortable or hungry or tired. She had not played with Pende or any of her other friends from Beriapi since June died.

Peter told her every night that they would leave soon. She did not complain or say much of anything to him, and he tried to get his understanding of her, the knowledge that she was suffering, out of his mind. In the last few days, Peter could not get away from his daughter's moods. Even when she was silent and in another room, her psyche was deafening, louder than his own soul.

He did not want to leave; he ignored Fitzroy's radio calls, imploring him to bring Taylor out of the field. He did not consider doing what Fitzroy asked. He could not even recall the man's face; the scientist had become an irritating, nagging voice in a far-away dream world. As the weeks passed, he saw only his daughter and Makino, the soft orange mud of the Abini roads, and the green sea of rain forest that covered Mt. Philip and Mt. Abini. He tried to dilute his being into the afternoon rains, the morning clouds that covered the eucalyptus, and the raggianas' shrieks that pierced through the forest's edges to the compound. Everything inside of him was diffused by the dense green of the mountains and the full moon's white light. He decided that he would never leave, and he pushed Boston and even Port Moresby and Goroka out of his mind.

When they stopped for a rest, Peter sat under a tamarind tree and fell asleep. He was exhausted from walking in the sun, and although he did not realize it until he woke up, he was dehydrated. Makino shook him, and Peter opened his eyes and felt the enormous thirst in his throat. He looked at the New Guinean who was leaning over him and then at his daughter. He looked around for June, expecting her familiar face and the blue bandanna covering her dark hair, but she was not there. He remembered where he was and then felt overwhelmed by June's absence. He blinked and stood up slowly. A memory of June in the dark hallway of their Boston apartment seeped into his mind, jarring him as he rose from the ground.

"Sorry," he said and clamped his hand on Makino's shoulder.

When they got to the compound, Peter lit the Colemans. His boots were encrusted with mud, and he left them on the stairs outside the front door. He filled the kettle and put it on the stove.

Makino sat on the floor and began building a fire in the oil-drum fireplace.

"*Masta Peta,*" he asked, "what are you going to do with the blood?"

Peter looked at Makino. How could he explain this?

"I'm going to make science with them," he said. He did not like the way that the English words and the Western concepts translated. Peter sat down at the table and smiled at Makino.

"I'm looking for what things are inside of people. Their blood tells me."

Makino nodded his head slowly. Peter waited for the New Guinean to say something and when he did not, Peter got up, lifted the kettle off the stove, and poured boiling water into the teapot.

"Some people think you are working poison," Makino said.

Peter placed the lid on the teapot and shook his head. He never really believed the fear of poison in Abini. It seemed impossible, put on. He had sat at the Abini and Malvi crossroads listening to twelve-hour arguments over poison magic and seen grown men scurrying home at twilight, rushing to avoid the dark, when they said that poison men were strongest. But he still did not think that the people here really, in their heart of hearts, believed it anymore than he did. It is a code, he thought, a metaphor for anger, aggression, and emotional attachments.

"No," he said to Makino, "I am not working poison with the blood."

Makino seemed remote and unsatisfied with his answer.

"*Wannim?*" Peter asked.

They could hear the stream flowing under the house and the wood crackle and spit in the fireplace.

"Everyone is worried about Misses June," he said.

Peter was impatient with Makino. He knew that every death in Abini was explained by poison and then fought over until the blame was assigned. When an infant in the village had died of malnutrition and dehydration, he and June went to the "court" and sat on the earth floor of Beriapi and listened, not understanding, to the grueling arguments, tears, and denials and watched as the baby's uncle was assigned blame and then humiliated and punished. It was too much for Peter to think that this was how the village was looking at June's death. He wanted to shake Makino, to push the superstition from his body.

Instead, he said, "My wife was a white woman. It's different for white people. We don't use poison magic. We can't die from poison."

Peter was exasperated that he had to pretend to believe in poison. Makino nodded his head. The three of them ate the tinned fish and rice that Makino cooked and formed into balls with his hands. When they finished, he rolled a cigarette and smoked it, looking into the oil-drum fireplace as the embers receded under a thick pile of ash. He said good-bye then and left. It was the first time since June died that he had not stayed and slept in the kitchen, on the floor in front of the fireplace.

Peter turned on the BBC World Service and listened to the broadcast as it wavered and hissed out of the receiver. He turned off the radio and stood in the door and looked out at the black night, tracing the red from the cooking fires inside the huts of Beriapi. He knew that Makino was disappointed with his explanation.

That night Peter dreamed a memory from a summer he spent in Maine with June before Taylor was born. They had bought lobsters in Castine and put them in a wooden trap in the bay, to keep them fresh until dinnertime. As Peter and June drank vodka tonics and watched the sunset, the lobsters were stolen by people from a yacht that had anchored thirty feet in front of their dock. In the dream Peter felt how he was drunk from the cocktails and tasted the ocean salt on his skin. He was helpless as the memory of June crying in the kitchen of their summer rental repeated, looping through his dream thoughts. Peter woke up disturbed and lay in bed, trying to banish the images that his unconscious had brought into his mind.

...

In the next few days Peter began to type up his handwritten field notes. He typed from after breakfast until the rain began, stopping only to make peanut butter sandwiches and tea for him and Taylor. He sealed the stacks of typed paper in plastic bags and decided to mail the notebooks to his parents for safekeeping.

The afternoon he finished typing, he began to worry about Taylor and called to her. She was outside feeding the chickens, and she came to the back door, the bread board stacked with chopped-up crumbs in her hands. Dozens of clucking chickens surrounded her, squawking and pecking at her bare feet.

"Come in here," he said.

She shrugged her shoulders and put the bread board down in the midst of the chickens. They descended upon the food, fighting each other, clucking, and his daughter walked up the stairs. Peter pointed at her feet. They were filthy, the pink skin caked in orange earth and chicken shit. He led her into the kitchen, and she sat down at the table. He filled a pan with water and Lux and began to wash her feet. He rubbed her ankles, her soles, and the delicate, dirty spaces between her toes. When he was done, the water was dark with dirt, and he took a tea towel and dried her off. He got hydrogen peroxide from the medicine box and cleaned the cuts on her feet, dabbing at the dirt with a cotton square.

"Now," he said, smiling, "just stay here until you dry."

He put his hand on her shoulder. Taylor's skin felt cold, and when she looked up at him, she seemed deliberately empty. As she stared, he became angry and imagined her beating heart contracting, expanding, and the strong gush of blood in her body. Her steady gaze made him guilty and then annoyed—she seemed judgmental and condescending, and he dreaded that this was how it would always be between them.

Peter looked around the kitchen at the orange oil-drum fireplace to the pushed-open window and then at the fiberglass sink with its spigot and rack full of drying dishes. He realized that he missed June, and the feeling stunned him with its intensity. He closed his eyes and thought of time going on, slowing everything down, washing the color out of the days. He saw that his research was fragmented. He hadn't found out anything, and he knew then that there wasn't anything to learn, only time to be spent in this place with its hallucinatory sun that streaked the sky with bleeding yellow light before the rains covered the earth.

...

Two days later Taylor and Makino followed Peter to the Abini river. When they got there, he set up three large rocks in an open triangle that formed a protected pooling of the cold, rushing water. He placed the blood samples in the deepest part of the pooling, digging the vials into the sandy riverbed. He was pleased that he thought to put the samples there. He put his hand in the cold Abini and held it under the water until his fingertips were numb.

"Who needs refrigeration?" he asked, grinning.

As the three of them walked away from the river, the rain started, mild at first. For a moment, Peter worried about the Abini swelling and washing his blood samples downstream. He watched Makino ahead of him, swinging his machete, clearing stray vines and branches from the path.

By the time they reached the main road, it was raining hard, soaking their hair and clothes. Peter took Taylor's hand in his. He was elated that the river was refrigerating the blood. He was immensely glad that his daughter was there with him, feeling the day end. He marveled that she did not look like him or June, and at that moment, with her hair wet and full of twigs and the dirt that covered her legs and arms, she was indistinguishable from the New Guinean landscape around him. He thought that she had absorbed the place, and he was proud of her. He smiled at her and began to recite in a loud voice,

> O camerado close! O you and me at last, and us two only.
> O a word to clear one's path ahead endlessly!
> O something ecstatic and undemonstrable! O music wild!
> O now I triumph—and you shall also . . .

Peter put his hand on his daughter's head, but she did not return his smile. He was embarrassed that she did not enjoy the poem. June would have liked it; she would have smiled at him reciting in the rain. He looked over at Makino, worried that he noticed Taylor's reaction, but the New Guinean stared straight ahead into the rain. She is only a girl, Peter thought, but he was disappointed.

They walked toward the compound, and rivulets of rainwater formed, carving narrow gutters in the road that flowed with sticks, leaves, and pebbles. Peter watched Taylor's yellow boots as she stepped into the clingy, muddy earth. When they climbed up the hill over the reach, he looked at thin columns of smoke seeping from the thatch roofs of Beriapi into the rain.

Taylor climbed over the compound fence, and the pink skin of her thighs was shocking against the wet green darkness of the path. Makino had insisted that they keep her with them all the time, although she did not want to go off on her own, anyway. In the first confusing days after June died, when Makino moved into the house, he whispered to Peter that there were boys, young men from Beriapi, the same ones that they had found her with before, that were hovering too close to the girl again.

Peter was not surprised, but it made him uncomfortable that the whole village knew that this was happening. He had learned that if one person in Abini knew anything, everyone knew. It made sense to him that Taylor would not understand boys who were being sexual. Why should she understand? This place, the dark earth, the gardens that were cut from rain forest, the smoke-filled thatch huts, this was real to her; his daughter did not know America, with its concrete playgrounds and rigid codas that delineated genitals from mouths with hysterical intensity, as anything more than a half-remembered dream. He decided then that he and Makino would protect her, and he liked the idea of the two of them as cofathers for the girl: one New Guinean, one American. He saw everything in its place.

He felt an enormous surge of affection as he watched his daughter, her green polka-dot dress wet and stuck to her skin, as she brushed past the poinsettia bushes. He wanted to reach out and hold her in his arms. It was still raining, and as he followed her, he thought that he couldn't send her to June's mother. She would do

the Queensland Correspondence School with him. He would teach
her to read and speak proper English and take her to Madang for
vacations, and she would swim in a chlorinated pool and drink Coca-
Cola and that would be her experience of Western marvels.

And then, when he finally got to the top of the path, his head
full of plans for Taylor, his eyes, mouth, and skin covered in the
climax of the late afternoon downpour, everything was askew. He
stood stunned, unable to read anything that he saw. He drank in
the scene, the woven-bamboo walls ripped apart, his possessions
covered in mud, the rain—the endless rain—washing everything
with brown and gray and black, but still he could not figure out
what was in front of him.

In the years that followed this day, when Peter could not stop
thinking about it, he would not be sure when he first saw what had
happened to the house. Was it when he thought about his daughter
and raised his eyes from the ground to try and see her? Or was it
when he had already crossed the grass lawn that fanned across the
compound like a ragged rug? But then, later, it seemed that the whole
day happened at once, that there was never a time when he did not
know what would occur. In fact, he would think that he knew about
his house when he was at the Abini river with Taylor and Makino;
that he felt its destruction like a long-separated twin feeling a twinge
and knowing that somewhere his brother was dead.

The two trees that stood to the east of the compound had fallen
over on top of the house, cleaving it open like a bird's belly sliced
while it was alive, its veins still pumping blood to quivering organs.
Peter stood staring at the storeroom's emptied shelves and the
twenty-pound canvas rice bag broken, the white grains bright against
the ground. He saw tins of Twinings, broken glass jars of Tiptree
jam, tubes of tomato paste, and the tins of spices labeled in June's
handwriting dispersed in the mud. For the first time since he had
been in the field he felt protective of his wife and her possessions.

Peter tried to move quickly across the compound, but the rain slowed his footsteps. His notes were scattered, the black ink of his kinship charts smeared by the rain. The Olivetti was yanked from its red plastic case and dumped into the hollow of the stream. Hundreds of Polaroid images of sober-faced Abini villagers were scattered on the broken woven-bamboo floor and the ground and covered in muddy footprints.

He heard screaming through the rain and saw his daughter, who had crawled under the split thatch of the roof into his bedroom. She was holding her doll and June's blue pajamas to her face.

"Come here!" he shouted, but she stayed put, rocking back and forth. Peter could not find the two-way radio, and he saw that the beds had been stripped of blankets and sleeping bags and the pillows were smeared in the mud.

The trees that bisected his house were wide, healthy, enormous trees. He was furious that the villagers would loot his house after a tree fell. But just then, as he looked around, he felt sick and knew exactly what had happened. The trees did not fall: they were cut with an ax. The wood at the base was as healthy and pink as his daughter's thighs. It was hewed into chips that covered the trees' base and the wet ground around them.

The interior of his house, the space that was off-limits to the entire village of Abini, was laid open, the possessions rifled through. He felt a wild adrenaline rush along his spine. He turned to Makino, waiting for him to speak. Unconsciously, Peter tilted his head to the side and bent down slightly, the way he always did when he talked to the shorter man. The rain was running down Peter's neck, under his clothes, and along his face. He felt that he would start shouting from its insistence, from the relentless tapping on his skull. He breathed in the wet earth smell and the sound of Taylor's crying and thought that he would drown from all the liquid in the air.

Peter watched Makino carefully now, regarding him as intently as he had ever looked at another human being. He wanted Makino to walk through the rain to his side. He saw Makino's face; his close-set eyes, the broad nose above wide lips. The New Guinean's gums were dyed red from chewing betel nut, and as he returned Peter's stare, his mouth was open as though he was just about to speak. The two men gazed at each other and said nothing. Peter looked away first, at his daughter, who was sitting on the broken floor, her legs dangling to the ground, holding her mother's pajamas to her body. His initial panic receded.

Makino's skin was glistening in the rain. His shorts and T-shirt were dark and colorless from the downpour. He stood there, motionless, and when Peter looked back at him, he saw that the man was mouthing words.

"Who did this?" Peter asked, excitedly. He couldn't control the tone in his voice. "Who?" he shouted.

Makino said nothing. Peter began chattering in Pisin.

"A rascal," he said, gesturing at the mess in front of them. "Some young men, some thieves did this."

Makino shrugged his shoulders so slightly that Peter almost missed the gesture. Peter was acutely aware of himself then, surrounded by the rain. He was pressing Makino, eager as a child to be reassured. He was mortified, as he began begging the New Guinean to tell him that everything was as it always was.

Makino said nothing. He stood there for a few minutes looking over the mess of the house, the possessions on the ground. He did not look at Taylor. After a while he walked away; he did not go toward the path because he would have had to pass Peter. Instead, he stepped over a torn woven-bamboo wall and passed by the chicken coop and then hopped over the fence into the scrub brush that surrounded the compound.

Peter couldn't believe that he was watching Makino leave. "You can't leave us!" he shouted into the rain.

He was furious. The anger seeped into his intestines and then through his belly and chest. He wanted to take Makino's face in his hands and ask him if he knew how ugly he was, how short, how his skin smelled foul and his breath stank from the rotting molars in his mouth. He thought then that Makino did not comprehend anything about the world, that he didn't sense who Peter was, how much more he had than everyone in Abini, or he wouldn't dare leave him at that moment. He felt that everything was happening as he knew it would, as he wished it wouldn't. He willed Makino to turn around, to come back and help them build a rain shelter and start a fire. I'm a child, he thought.

"It's so stupid," he said in English to the vision of Makino's form disappearing. "It's too stupid to even talk about."

Peter turned around and stared at his house. He was not afraid. He knew that Fitzroy would send a helicopter when he didn't raise them on the radio. And he knew that the villagers would not even come to say good-bye when the helicopter arrived. For a moment he was full of pity for Taylor and himself. It occurred to him that she knew this was coming, she understood it for weeks, and that was why she had stayed away from her friends. Her friends, he thought. He and June had not even left her her friends.

The darkening sky was still full of rain, and Mt. Abini's thick forest was covered in the dense blue cloud of evening. Peter anticipated the scenery before he shifted his gaze to it, and he realized that everything that surrounded him was familiar. He had finally absorbed the landscape.

The sun was setting, and cold mountain air flowed into the valley. He felt an ache, as though a memory, just below the surface of his consciousness, was haunting him. Although no one would understand him when he said it in the future, he knew that there was nothing in this place. He bent down to feel the muddy ground. The cold earth was saturated with tapeworm larvae and grass seed that he had bought at Steamships, and he rubbed it on his forehead and cheeks and lips. Eventually, the rain washed this dirt from his face.

EIGHTEEN

A mass of gardenia, frangipani, and bougainvillea grows in front of the house that Peter rented on Half Moon beach. In the morning, when Taylor leaves for school in her starched white shirt and polyester kilt, she sidesteps the blossoms and green leaves that sprawl across the porch. From the bus stop the house looks disheveled with overgrown flowers, and when Taylor is on the bus, driving away, she often cannot distinguish the building from the plants that grow around it.

Peter is awake when his daughter leaves; he watches her walk away. The white socks that she has pulled up to her knees and her patent leather shoes gleam in the morning light. He makes coffee and toast for himself, putting his breakfast on the crumb-covered plate his daughter has left behind. He reads a book, sips coffee, and then goes for a run, jogging along the sandy road that follows the curve of the beach, past houses, palm trees, and rotting fences that stand in front of empty lots that were cleared of buildings by ferocious coastal storms. He turns back when the tarmac dead-ends into a patch of Queensland rain forest, gulping air into his cherry-pink face.

In the afternoons, before Taylor comes home, he reads, writes letters, and drives the white Toyota into Cairns to shop at the outdoor market. The income from his wife's estate allows him to buy whatever he wants there: passion fruit, herbs, fresh vegetables, and tender lamb chops every day.

When his daughter walks off the school bus, he has already lit the charcoal and is preparing lamb, or salmon, or crab legs for the barbecue. He has bought dozens of cookbooks and is teaching himself how to make exquisite food. He spends the hours alone chopping vegetables, deboning the delicate flesh of fish, and tying leeks around roasted wild mushrooms with slender chives. The dishes he proffers to his eight-year-old daughter are as complex as landscape paintings.

The money is the girl's. Although she does not understand what it means that she has so much, she knows exactly how things are different between her and her father from when her mother was alive. He is deferential, permissive, and withdrawn from her. When she is an adolescent, she will obsessively read the lives of the Tudor princes and princesses and recognize her life with her father in these stories of childhoods surrounded by courtiers.

For a week, an enormous frog, with neon-green, pimply skin, that has yellow eyeballs as big as marbles, travels through the house. It makes its way from the scraggly regrowth rain forest behind them, across the living room to Half Moon beach every day. The frog grasps the window louvers with its large, sloppy toes and leans back, staring at the father and daughter as they inhabit the small house, quietly avoiding each other, intent on causing no offense. The frog wakes Taylor up in the middle of the night, perched above her bed, its yellow gaze scanning her from head to foot. She does not scream when it appears over her, pulling her out of a dream, nor is she moved when she sees that it has been flattened by a car. When she sees her father on the road, crying for the dead frog, she retreats into her room, waiting for an hour until she comes out to watch television.

The father and daughter live like this. Taylor gradually makes friends at the school. Her accent is wearing off; she has stopped thinking in Abini and is learning to read and write English. Her shoes do not constrain her anymore, and the soles of her feet have become soft and pink. Eventually, Beriapi and Mt. Abini become as remote as long forgotten dreams.

It was only once, when she was with her father in the Cairns marketplace, that everything was right before her: three Trobriand Island women, who were tall, with large afros, wearing bright, clean, *meri* blouses, walked through stalls that were overflowing with giant vegetables and tropical fruit, buying yams and mangoes. These women spoke Pisin and even smelled of Papua New Guinea as they walked past father and daughter. Although they looked nothing like Highlanders, Peter and Taylor stood staring, rooted to the spot, as if enchanted by the diffuse light that passed through the market's green fiberglass roof.

When Peter said hello and spoke to them in Pisin, the Trobriand Islanders only looked at him and turned away without a greeting, unwilling to exchange words with a white man. After the women walked away, Peter's Pisin stayed in the air, refusing to dissolve, and the familiar sounds were awkward between him and his daughter. At home that afternoon, Taylor went to her room and stared at pictures of June that her grandmother had sent her. She tried to pick out her features from her mother's face but could not.

When she thinks of her mother now, she can only remember the dark-colored wood of the funeral home, the car fumes that made her vomit when she walked through Boston, and her grandmother's perfumey smell as she pressed Taylor into her breasts and cried and whispered, "Please, stay with me, Taytie."

But Taylor could not imagine leaving her father. And when they got to Cairns, her father rewarded her for her presence, mistaking it for loyalty. He took her on a glass-bottomed boat that skirted the turquoise water of the Great Barrier Reef, and the two of them watched the impossible colors of the swaying coral and bright fish that darted away from the boat's engine.

However, Taylor is wary of her father. Most of the time when he talks to her, she pulls down a wall so thick that she hears him only slightly. But then, when he feeds her his extravagant meals, she feels the sharp taste of garlic and the lush meat of fresh tomatoes and is glad they are together.

In the evenings, Peter smokes hash and goes for walks on Half Moon beach. He asks Taylor to come with him on these journeys into the night that are full of moisture-heavy air and the sounds of salt water smashing on the shore, but she refuses. Instead, as soon as he leaves, she sits on a chair on the front porch and looks at the ocean. She watches the Pacific, scanning the Papuan Gulf. In those hours, while she gazes into the forever of waves and dark sky, she is waiting for a sign from her mother, for a sign from Abini. Her mind is still as she looks out, and she only occasionally sighs or shifts in the chair. Soon she will realize that nothing will ever come for her.